MW01233444

Stories on Love and Redemption

Edited by Cedric Harris

Saadia Ali Aschemann
Diane Dorce'
R. Fitzgerald
April C. Hayes
D.R. Johnson
Cordenia Paige
Torrance Stephens PhD.

Graphic cover and design by Denea Marcel

ISBN -13- 978-0-9774126-4-8

Library of Congress Control Number: 2007940926
Cover Art and Design by Denea Marcel
http://thegallerymarcel.blogspot.com

Published by FireFly Publishing & Entertainment

Printed in the United States by Morris Publishing
3212 East Highway 30
Kearney, NE 68847
1-800-650-7888

Why Bloggers' Delight...

When people ask us why we titled this book Bloggers' Delight, our first impulse is to pause, because we figure they probably "don't get it" and then secondly we smile, because it gives us the opportunity to talk about two of our passions: blogging and writing.

This book is a celebration of both. It is about the talent we get to experience week after week as we make our journey from one web log (blog) to the next. And, it is about embracing blogging as an effective tool to improve upon one's writing.

Bloggers' Delight, the name, also represents a change in the approach to the craft. The name itself is a derivation of The Sugar Hill Gang's album, *Rappers' Delight*. The rappers of their day embraced the art form for the pure love of it. They were innovators. They didn't want to follow the crowd just to get paid. We are emulating that example.

The authors in this project were chosen because they weren't looking to cash in on the latest trend. They write out of the sheer delight of the art form. They write because it is an essential part of who they are. So this project was created to help fuel that spirit within them.

The goal of Bloggers' Delight is to "change the game...one volume at a time." We do that, by bringing you fresh new voices found in the blogosphere. We do that, by being true to the Creator within us. Out of that sincerity you get to experience our literary love letters. Therefore, Bloggers' Delight is more than a book. It is a life line, and we hope you enjoy reading...through the lines.

Table of Contents

FOREWORD

Bloggers' Delight Origins

Written by

CapCity (Blog persona of Cordenia Paige)

Vibes. Music. Rhythm. Such forces have determined the destinies of people for centuries. I began blogging in order to open my heart and thoughts to a world of people unknown to me. Blogging was my way of coming out of the creative closet where I held my dear works of art very close, in danger of smothering them. As I ventured into the veritable blog-forest, I found myself drawn repeatedly to several blogs.

The Rich House (R. Fitzgerald) gave off an authoritative, no nonsense, and honest vibe. I enjoyed the commentary and variations of topics covered at *The Rich House*. It was a pleasant surprise that the male-run blog touched on Christian themes without being preachy and there was little mention of sports, which was also refreshing to me. I sent an email to the host of *The Rich House* inquiring about how to be added to his blog-roll. The patience that came across in his reply served to further endear me.

Write for Life initially drew me because of the name alone. I connected immediately with the need to write for life, as one needs to breathe. The host of *Write for Life's* southern genteelness and hospitality reverberated throughout her post topics and comments. I learned that it is possible to feel touched by the spirit of another whom I'd never met by interacting with *Write for Life's* host, MizRepresent (Diane Dorce´). She became one of the best friends I'd never met.

I was honored when the host of *The Rich House* approached me to ask if I would join him and several other bloggers on a writing journey toward publication. I learned that we were all children who came of age as Hip-Hop was born. Therefore, we bonded in more than writing. We shared a love for similar music, too. When *Bloggers' Delight* was suggested as the title of our collection, it "clicked" as a natural choice. We will set the precedence for the blog community as Rappers' Delight did for Hip Hop. For the most part, blogging is underground in the sense that only those who blog know what a web log is. By publishing written works of individuals who met in the blog-o-sphere, *Bloggers' Delight* will expose society's mainstream to the mysterious world of blogging. Yes, *"well, it's on-n-on-n-on-on-n-on, the beat don't stop until the break of dawn."*

Secret Garden

The promise of me
    has so much power
A magic key
    at this dark hour
Self-deprecating
    I dismiss
Calculating
    he insists
I can own him, I think
    with a suggested fantasy
A long lashed wink
    well cultivated beauty
Unlocking the solid gate
    to my secret garden
Unsettled, he can not wait
    let me in, he pleads, _again_
                again

Saadia Ali Aschemann

Dedication

Thanks to the Creator for my parents: Sarah and Conan, you are my greatest inspirations! I greatly appreciate R. Fitzgerald for inviting me to this project and Diane for her encouragement along the way☺.

Rey of Hope
By Cordenia Paige

Antoine twirled his date on the dance floor and savored the view of her tight thighs as the yellow halter dress flared for his pleasure. In a very few hours those same thighs would be wrapped around his waist. He told his manhood to be patient: *No embarrassing me here, now!* Antoine smiled as her ample bosom pressed softly against his chest after this siren spun back to him. Swinging and spinning hand in hand, they hand-danced expertly in true D.C. fashion to the groove. She flashed that stunning bright smile at him. Her hazel eyes coyly met his in an obviously practiced manner. Antoine could care less that he had not been and probably would not be the only one "up in her" this week; all he wanted was his chance to dip in it tonight.

The song drew to an end and he led her off the dance floor. After paying the bar tab and heading toward the exit, Antoine proudly walked behind her as other men unabashedly admired her bountiful figure in passing. One or two even gave him "the nod and wink", the visual approval equivalent to 'dap': that knuckle-to-knuckle greeting among male comrades. Antoine was feeling that

1991 was a great year to be a straight, Black man in the nation's capital. He was young, fun and full of... himself.

As they strolled hand in hand to his black Mazda RX-7 parked across from the club on 12th and K Street, Antoine thought he heard someone call his name, but he was focused on *the matters at hand.* Just as he settled her into the passenger's side and headed around to the driver's side, he looked up to see his brother walking towards him.

"Wha's up, Corey? What you doin' out here this late, man?" Antoine slapped his brother's outstretched hand and pulled him in for a quick hug.

"Just leaving the office." Corey shrugged.

"It's almost midnight. But, you know what you do is your business."

Corey smirked, "You know I don't roll like that. We got a big case coming up. Shit, I really have more work to do, but I gotta get home to my Lena. Speaking of, who's the young lady, and why're you being rude?"

Corey cut his eye disapprovingly as he leaned down and extended his hand in through the driver's side, "How you doin'? I'm Corey."

"Sheila. Nice to meet you," She cooed and smiled.

"Likewise." Corey stood back up to his full 6'2" frame and looked Antoine in the eye. "Well, Li'l Bruh. I'm going home to my wife. Y'all be easy."

"Aiight, man. I'll see you at Ma's on Sunday."

Antoine sighed and rolled his eyes as he settled behind the wheel. He knew by Corey's look that he was gonna get beef on Sunday, no matter what their mother had on the menu.

"You alright, Boo?" Sheila asked stroking the back of Antoine's head and neck.

Antoine looked down at her and the promise of *all to come--literally*--shook off his brother's judgmental expression and grinned. "Yea, Sexy. Everything is 'kool and the gang.'" He started the engine, put the car into gear and headed toward her place--sliding his hand beneath her dress and between her thighs.

***

"What the hell are you thinking?" Corey whispered into the phone. Though he was in his office, Corey kept his voice low because his secretary often came into his office without advance notice when he was handling a seriously important case. But, he felt the need to take the time to call his brother and get this off his chest. This could not wait until Sunday's dinner.

Antoine was on his way home and he did not want to hear this now. He didn't want to hear it at all, really, so he figured he might as well get it over with. Maybe, if he was lucky, this early call meant that Corey wouldn't bring it up in front of the family.

"*What*, man? Why you trippin'? You act like I'm stepping out on *you*. Damn! Is this what marriage does to a man: take his balls?"

"You lucky I'm at work. All I'm sayin' is in a way you are stepping out on me. I'm the one who hooked you up with Reyna, remember? So, you know who gets the backlash? See, I should've known better. I thought you were ready to chill with one steady sistah."

"I do want one steady chick for public affairs. Look here, Big Bruh, you know I'm not getting married anytime soon if that's what you're crying about. Hell, I'm sure Reyna knows it, too."

Corey inhaled slowly and exhaled as he calmed himself. "Look, man, you been seeing Reyna almost a year, now. Y'all are in your mid-twenties...and you don't think she's hanging in here for marriage? You really don't know women, do you? You've got to break it off with her and *now*. I will not stand by and watch you do this to Reyna, and if Lena finds out that I actually *know* you're cheating on her... Let's just say the Sistah-hood is going to come down on me hard. Maaannn, Reyna's really good people, and she deserves a brother who will appreciate more than her regular willingness to be at your beck and call."

"I can't break up with her now, Corey. We're going out tonight. Maybe after Sunday dinner it'll be easier."

"Antoine, if Reyna shows up for dinner this Sunday, I'm going to tell her in front of the entire family. I know that would crush her, but I'm tired of you doing this to women. After Reyna, I won't care anymore. She was your nephew's first grade teacher, for Chrissakes! I thought she could turn even a knucklehead like you around. She's smart, fine as hell, and will make a great mother."

"Damn, Bruh, it sounds like you had a crush on Ms. Crabtree your dayum self." Antoine hoped his remark would get Corey to lighten up. It didn't.

"Didn't you learn anything from Daddy's bullshit? Women today don't stick with you like that. If Ma were thirty years younger she would've been left Daddy, taken his kids and emptied his bank account. Save yourself and Reyna some headache. End it tonight...*before* you hit it. Can you do me that favor? Leave the woman with some shred of dignity. From here on, I'll stay out of your social affairs."

"Bet. If this will get you to leave me alone, consider it ended."

"Thanks, Antoine. I'll holla at you later; the shit's about to hit the fan up in here with this workload."

"Cool, I'll see you later, Big Bruh."

Antoine clicked the end button on his cell phone with slight attitude. He was on his way home from Sheila's, and the last thing he had wanted to hear was his brother giving him grief about Reyna or anything else. He needed to shower again and get dressed to meet downtown with one of his real estate clients. Antoine sighed heavily and realized he was relieved. He had tried to keep his side women away from his family, but got too comfortable. Antoine knew Corey's law firm was near that spot last night, but figured it was way past the time when anyone with a day job would be out during the week. Honestly, Antoine knew it was time to break it off with Reyna, anyway. She was a sweet heart, but he had gotten complacent with her. His family loved her, so it made it easy to have her around them. Scrolling through his Rolodex mentally, Antoine decided that Sheila might be up for being his public showpiece. At least with her there would be no strings attached. She definitely knew what time it was.

Antoine waited to call Sheila once he got to his apartment. She wasn't worth the minutes on his cell phone.

"Hey, Sweet Thang."

"Hey, Big Daddy. You coming back for round five before lunch?"

He chuckled at her insatiable appetite as he smoothly arranged his follow up to what he knew would be melodrama with Reyna. "Naw, sweetie. I just found out I have to work late tonight. They're stressing me at work, and I was wondering if you'd be up for some de-stressful therapy when I finished up. But, I wanted to make sure it's okay because it might be really late, and I don't want to call you too late."

"You just bring your hard leg over here when you're finished, and Mama Sheila will work out the kinks for ya."

Antoine hung up smiling; it was indeed the right time to break it off with Reyna.

\#   \#   \#

Sitting in front of her apartment building in the car with Antoine, Reyna tried to catch her breath. She touched the button, which electronically slid the window down on the passenger's side. Reyna took in a deep breath hoping it would calm her or cool her off. It didn't. She tried to refocus, as Antoine asked her, "You do understand, right? I'm just not ready to give you what you ought to have. You deserve a good brother ... who wants to commit to you fully."

She stared into his eyes that seemed to plead with her to understand. Reyna took in all of his wonderful features one last time. The full lips, she had enjoyed nibbling, while the tickle of his neatly trimmed mustache and beard thrilled her. His thick eyebrows above the dark brown eyes had made her melt every time they grazed over her. Reyna wondered how a man as handsome and caramel smooth as Antoine could suddenly take on the gargoyle-like qualities that she saw now. She wanted nothing more than the satisfaction of digging her well-manicured, conservatively cut fingernails deeply into his face, scarring him for life, as she felt his words were doing to her.

Instead, Reyna dropped her eyes and smoothed the hem of her silky, floral dress over her knee as she tried to wrap her brain around the news that Antoine was sending. Was it her imagination that they'd just had an amazing night of dinner and dancing? In her head, she chanted, "Do NOT let him see you cry. Do NOT cry in front of him!" Aloud, Reyna's voice quivered slightly as she asked, "What is it that makes you think I want such a binding commitment? I never mentioned marriage to you; your mother said she wanted us to be married--not me."

"I guess that's just it. My parents think you'd make the perfect daughter-in-law. I don't want to be married anytime soon, so I don't want to lead you on. I don't want my parents' wishes to lead you on or to pressure me. I really like you, and I don't want to hurt you."

Too late for that! Reyna thought as she bit her lip, gathered her wrap, her purse and her pride. She shakily reached for the handle to get out of the car. She knew that at any moment she would not have control over the floodgates that were wavering.

"You're cool? You're going to be alright?" Antoine asked as he reached out to touch her shoulder.

Reyna recoiled as the door and her anger released. "I have to be. You weren't the first. Now, you won't be the last." She slapped him with those harsh words in an attempt to mask her level of devastation. Reyna wanted to sling one of her lavender pumps at him, but refused to give him any satisfaction that he had hurt her so deeply. In an effort to regain her composure she caught the car door, which she was initially tempted to slam. Instead, she closed it quietly and walked blindly to her apartment building without daring to look back.

She didn't even care that the elderly couple in the elevator looked at her quizzically as she began to bawl uncontrollably up to her apartment on the 8th floor. The old lady patted her arm, "Remember that joy comes in the morning, sweetie." Reyna gave a watery smile and nodded as they got off on the 5th floor.

Reyna wallowed in the release that she got from crying through most of the night, but hated the after effects of swollen, red eyes and a red nose. She chuckled sarcastically to herself when she leaned on the sink and looked into the mirror the morning after Antoine broke off their almost yearlong relationship. "Well, at least he had the decency to break up with me at the start of the weekend, so I have time to get my face together before I have to see my students. What the hell am I going to do today? I can't go anywhere looking like a gila monster." After tending to her morning needs, Reyna poured herself a tall glass of grapefruit juice. Grapefruit juice always made Reyna feel like she could tackle the day. But, as she sat on the sofa and looked out her living room window down 16th street, she knew it would take more than grapefruit juice *this* morning.

"Who do I call first?" Reyna asked herself even as she started dialing her mother's number.

"Good morning!" Mrs. Seaton was a morning person, and her cheery voice seemed to be the undoing of Reyna, who thought she couldn't cry anymore. "Oh, my lord. Who is this? What in heaven's name is the matter?"

"Ma, it's me--Reyna. I didn't mean to start crying all over again."

"What's the matter, baby girl?" Reyna could hear the concern in her mother's voice and imagine the pained expression on her face.

Reyna took a deep breath and tried to speak without bawling again, which seemed more and more impossible. Her words came between shaky breaths "Antoine...he doesn't want to be...with me anymore."

Reyna wished that she were lying in her mother's arms as she heard her whisper, "Oh, baby...I'm so sorry. Do you want to come over? Want me to fix you a nice, hot meal?"

"I can't get it together to leave out today, Ma" Reyna's voice gathered a bit more strength since the worst part of the telling was over. "I just wanted you to be the first to know. I'm probably going to sleep most of today."

"You sure you don't want me to send Rondel up there with a plate of food?"

Reyna had to smile at the suggestion. She knew her mother must have been feeling her pain because her mother's philosophy was that a good, hearty meal solved most of life's ailments. Her mother also knew that Reyna's older brother, Rondel always could bring a shine to Reyna's eyes. "Yea...okay, if you can. Can you also ask him to spring for a nice bottle of Shiraz? But don't tell him what happened, yet. I don't want him to come through the door like gangbusters ready to go on a manhunt."

"I won't. I'll just tell him you're a little under the weather. Did you call your daddy and tell him?"

"Not yet. I'll call him later tonight, once I've calmed down. I don't want Daddy to rally Rondel up into a posse."

Mrs. Seaton sighed, "I'm glad to hear you smiling through your pain, baby girl. It may take a little while, but the Seatons are strong people so you gonna be all right."

"Thanks, Ma."

Needing someone else to talk to, she dialed her best friend, Sydnee.

"Hey, mamacita! How was the hot new spot, Republic Gardens? That is where Antoine took you last night, right?

Glad that her tear ducts seemed empty, Reyna responded, "It was the perfect place for a perfect ending to a perfect relationship."

"Hold up! What are you talking about, Reyna?"

"Last night after having such a great time, Antoine, just...broke it off."

"Girl, I'm on my way over there. This is not a conversation that we can have on the phone. Do you have anything in that bat-cave to eat? Never mind, I'll bring a few groceries so we can fix breakfast and mimosas. I need a drink to hear this. And I know you haven't eaten a thing."

Reyna just smiled as Sydnee rambled on. Sydnee was a nurse by trade and loved taking care of others. She was a natural at sensing the needs of others and providing just the right level of comfort with a dash of tough love. Reyna took a shower and steeled herself for the visit of Hurricane Sydnee.

Thirty minutes later, Reyna was feeling fresh, albeit still sluggish. She had donned her comfiest attire: black yoga pants, a faded pink, soft, brushed cotton v-neck tank top and ballerina slippers. It was the type of outfit she felt decent in with close friends, but could also curl up on the sofa as she was, flipping through a magazine while waiting for Sydnee who would arrive at any moment.

Sydnee whirled into Reyna's place by noon, carrying several bags of groceries, including two bottles of great champagne, freshly squeezed orange juice and strawberries. As Reyna helped unpack the bags, she looked forward to Sydnee's perfect mimosas. Though a mimosa is a simple concoction, Sydnee knew the secret to the right mix of champagne and orange juice. Her mimosas went down smoothly and left their "victims" with a wonderful afterglow. While they worked side by side in Reyna's kitchen, Sydnee got straight to the point. "What in God's name did Antoine give as his excuse for breaking off your perfect relationship as he broke your heart in one fell swoop?"

Reyna smiled. She knew that Sydnee was being overly dramatic in attempt to keep it light so Reyna wouldn't completely collapse from heartache. "According to him, I deserve better than he has to offer. I deserve to be with a man who will fully commit to marriage and me. He was feeling pressured by his family." Reyna took a deep breath as she completed that mini-monologue in one breath. She paused from cracking eggs into the bowl so she could cut her eye at Sydnee, who stopped cutting the stems off of the freshly washed strawberries long enough to put her hand on one hip and stare at her.

"Okay, Rey, you're my girl--so know that everything I say today I say with love towards you--but are you fuckin' kiddin' me? It took that muthafuckah almost a year to realize he wasn't *good* enough for you and to feel pressured by his family? Why da hell did he take you to meet his parents in the first place? Oh, I forgot--because his brother introduced the two of you. Then why da hell didn't he end it sooner? Or better yet, the fool should've told his brother he didn't want to meet anyone worthy of relationships; just take him to the local strip joint, where he could have his pick. That sorry ass excuse for a man knew good 'n' damn well that he didn't want a long term relationship from jump street."

Reyna was torn between laughing at how indignant Sydnee was and crying at the truth that she spouted. She felt delirious as she giggled while adding grated cheese to the eggs. "I know I am really as much to blame. If I'm honest with myself, really honest, I knew all along that Antoine was a restless spirit. I guess I should be thankful that he did finally man-up and break it off at all instead of bringing home some shit he didn't leave here with. But, dayum--I'm going to miss our early morning sessions. Sydnee girl, that fool could put it *down!*"

"Ooooh, so here I am thinking you're gonna toss yourself out the window because this clown broke your heart...when the real truth is you're bad as Richard Pryor: you can leave, just don't take the dick!"

They both paused in the meal preparation and laughed until tears ran from their eyes.

The two of them settled down with their plates of omelettes, toast and home-fried potatoes. Reyna returned to the kitchen to get glasses, the chilled pitcher of mimosa and the bowl of strawberries. Once that was placed in an easy to reach position on her glass coffee table, Reyna flopped beside Sydnee onto the plush, red sofa with a huge sigh.

"You know, Syd, as much as I knew that Antoine was seeing other women, I kept hoping that his family would help him to understand how good we were for each other. I thought maybe he'd realize how much I had his back and had more to offer than the other chicks he met. I loved his family so much and will miss them more than anything. No, I'll miss him and his buffoonery, too. We had some really good times. That was the problem. Our only problem was that he would never commit. I tried to be the girl who never tripped out about that. I didn't want to be a nagging girlfriend; I wanted him to feel like I was as cool as one of his boys. I'm just so angry with myself for getting caught up emotionally like this."

Sydnee swallowed a mouthful of potatoes. "So, you two never talked about the status of your relationship or where you wanted it to go?"

"Not really. I didn't want to be the one to bring it up. I knew he would think I was trying to pressure him into something that he wasn't ready for." Reyna picked at her plate, nibbling a bit of the omelette. She knew she needed to eat but didn't have much of an appetite.

"Hmmm, well, if you never talked about what you wanted from the relationship, I guess he's not such a clown after all."

Reyna poured a mimosa for herself and refreshed Sydnee's. As she dropped a strawberry into the glasses, she asked. "What do you suggest? I mean, I'm twenty-six. I don't want men to think I'm pressed to be married."

"Well, since I'm three years older than you, guys may think I'm pining for marriage since I'm at thirty's doorstep. But, I still like the straight up approach. Right now, I don't want marriage, and I'm not looking for commitment. I let brothers know that upfront."

"I don't know, Syd. I like regular intimacy with one man and that's more than just sex."

Sydnee placed her half-finished plate of food onto the coffee table and picked up her drink. "In an ideal world, I'd like that, too. But until then, I'll settle for an honest booty call with no strings attached. I have two brothers who I'm comfortable with calling on. If I can't reach one, the other is bound to be available. They strap up when I need my back scratched, and everyone goes home happy--no lies told. If you want marriage, what's so bad about letting brothers know that in the beginning?"

"Girllll, please. You know how quickly brothers here in DC run from the M word--especially in our age bracket. Not to mention the fact that brothers here have their pick of women tossing themselves at them."

"I don't know, Rey, I think you're putting more on yourself than you need to. At the very least, it sounds like you're scaring yourself more than necessary. Try this for a while: when you meet a new brother, work it into one of your first five conversations that you're looking to be married by the time you're thirty-five. You should do an experiment. Keep a little notebook of the next few men you meet. Jot down their names and the reactions that you get when you tell them that you want to be married. I can't imagine they'll all bolt for the exit. I would say let's start tonight, but I have a late shift to pull."

"Good...because I'm in no shape emotionally nor physically to be going anywhere tonight. I refuse to go up in anybody's party with my eyes all puffy and red."

Sydnee laughed, "Chil' please, that'll help you get a brother who's in search of a damsel in distress. You gotta learn to work what 'cho mama gave ya!" She drained her mimosa, stood, and stretched her 5'11" frame. "Now that I know you'll be fine, I'm going to carry my rusty dusty home and get ready for work. If I'm lucky, I'll get Bruce to come over for a quickie. All this talk about men has me hot and bothered."

Reyna shook her head. "Well so much for sympathy from you. Rub it in that you still gettin' it on the regular."

Sydnee ran her fingers through her shoulder length bob then smirked at Reyna. "If you just want it on the regular, I can introduce you to Bruce's friends, and you can see which one you like. He has some cute friends who I'm wondering about myself, but you know "The Code" won't let you do your man's friends...even if he's not really your man."

"Thanks, but no thanks." Reyna said as she stood and began to gather up items to return them to the kitchen. She and Sydnee carried all of the breakfast items to the kitchen, scrapped off the plates and put uneaten food items into the refrigerator.

"Well, let me use the powder room before I run," Sydnee announced, leaving Reyna alone to her thoughts and the dishwasher that she was loading.

Sydnee returned to find Reyna staring out the kitchen window. "You are going to be okay, aren't you? I can call in sick, if you need me to hang out with you."

"Yea, I'll be fine." Reyna brushed her hands over her short, Anita Baker-inspired hair cut. "Besides, Ma's sending Rondel over later with my dinner."

"That's good. Tell that man he's the one I let get away. I'm not getting married until his wife tosses him out into the streets for me to rescue." Sydnee laughed.

"Yea, we know that's about as likely to happen as Jesse Jackson talking without rhymes. I don't know where Rondel and his wife come from, but it ain't natural for couples to get along that well."

They both laughed as Reyna walked Sydnee to the door. "Let me know if you want to go to Tyson's Corner after church tomorrow. I could use a li'l shoe therapy and my face won't be swollen anymore."

"Alright, Super Soul Sistah. I'll call you tomorrow after choich!" Sydnee stated after they hugged and she stepped into the hall. "Keep your head up!"

Reyna pulled out her buddy, her journal, to which she turned in times of great cheer or great need:

"Well, journal, here I am again. Talking to you about relationships and self-ships (my new word for relating to ones' self☺). Antoine ended our relationship last night. I haven't talked to Rita yet because I don't want to hear my big sister go into her negative diatribe about what's not happening with brothers of today. I have enough of that inside me already that I'm trying to flush out. I don't need to hear hers, too. I have to work at keeping myself enthused without hearing others bitch and moan.

Time to ask myself the questions that I hate to look at in Essence magazine: If there are activities that I like to enjoy with someone special--why not begin to enjoy them alone? Why not go for walks on Roosevelt Island alone (there are times when there are plenty of people out so it'll be safe)? Consider going to plays, museums and even take trips alone. The Smithsonian offers interesting tour-guided group trips. It's time to begin to enjoy life more fully solo because there's no guarantee that another person will enjoy all of the same activities that I enjoy. In the event that I am so lucky to marry the man of my dreams, there are going to be times when I'm alone, and I will need to practice amusing myself. Remember: I must be at peace with myself before I can truly enjoy the intimate company of another.

Yep. All of this Fabulous-Essence-Strong-Black-woman-psycho-babble sounds great. But, Gawwwwddddd, this HURTS! Please help me, God, to get through this...I

*don't even know what to call this. Is it a phase; will this
fear of being alone end with the new moon? Is this fear of
being alone simply because Antoine doesn't want me? Will I
meet another man who makes me smile as he did?
Jeeeeessssuuuusss! I don't want to cry anymore. I don't
know if I can cry anymore. Maybe I'll put on some shades
and go for a long walk. I think that'll help. If I stay in this
apartment until Rondel gets here, I'll probably polish off
that second bottle of champagne and that's not good."*

Reyna put her journal away, changed into a tee
shirt that provided more coverage, put on her sneakers and
then called her mom before heading out the door.

"Hey, Ma!"

"Hi Dahlin'! You sound much better. How you
feeling?"

"I'm fine, I just wanted to let you know I'm going to
go run a few errands, but I'll be back by six. Is that alright?

"Yea, baby girl. I'm almost done cooking dinner, but
I'll tell Rondel when he gets here that you'll be out for a
bit. He can help me fix some things here, anyway."

"Good. You better take advantage since you were
able to pull him away from Debra. And on a Saturday!"
They both chuckled.

"And I'm glad you're going to get some air instead of
staying by yourself pining away over that boy."

Reyna headed north on 16th street, crossed over
and walked into the southwest entrance of Meridian Hill
Park, also known as Malcolm X Park. It was one of the
most beautiful parks making a comeback in DC. Black
people frequented Meridian Hill Park for picnics and
picture-taking when Reyna's parents were young in the
Forties and Fifties. After the riots of the Sixties through
the crack-infested Eighties, most parks became drug dens.
In addition to the drug trade, Meridian Hill Park also

became a playground for homosexual interludes. The developers' collective greed saddened Reyna as she watched building after building in her neighborhood being refurbished and turned into condominiums. Many of the original Black residents could no longer afford to live in the area. She was glad to see the revitalization of the area but sad that it meant so many were misplaced. Reyna prayed that she would be able to afford to purchase if her building went condo.

Today, she tried not to focus too much on the variations of sadness around her. She simply wanted to soak up sunshine and thoroughly enjoy it as she walked up the wide steps on the west side of the waterfall pool that flowed through the lower half of Meridian Hill Park. When she got to the top of the steps, Reyna looked out over downtown DC with its visible monuments and took a deep breath as if she could draw DC into her lungs. She turned toward the north and the activity in the park on this warm May afternoon. There were Caribbean and Latino men playing soccer on the main lawn surrounded by some women whose children were running to and fro. There was a gathering near the middle section of the Promenade, off to the left side, of brothers with African drums. Reyna stopped for a minute near the drummers to watch and allow the beats of the drums to fill her spirit. She wished she could drum out the pain she felt. She chuckled to herself, "Maybe I'll get a drum to beat when I'm frustrated. I'm sure my neighbors would love *that*."

Reyna continued on northward through the park and exited by way of the northwest entrance just across the street from the Howard University dormitory that is named after the park. To get her blood flowing, Reyna increased her pace north to Columbia Road where she turned left and headed into the closest thing DC had to El Barrio. Reyna enjoyed the cultural feast where Latin "tiendas" dominated, while a few African restaurants and shops flourished.

"Hola, Señor Santiago!" Reyna called out as she entered one of her favorite little corner stores. "Tiene algunas platanos negro, hoy?" She felt comfortable practicing her Spanish with the Santiagos.

"Yes, we got good plantains today. Dark and sweet as you like them, Ms. Seaton. How you been? Has some man been keeping you too busy for us?"

Reyna smiled knowing that he had no idea how he'd slid another spur into her aching heart. Mr. Santiago always teased her about men in her life so she brushed off her own present state of angst and changed the subject. "More like mucho trabajo! How is Señora Santiago?"

"The Mrs. is fine. She's out spending my money today! What is this about too much work? A beautiful young woman like you should have plenty of men who work for you. So, you can be like Mrs. Santiago--out enjoying the sunshine while her poor husband slaves away."

"I'll remember your words of wisdom, Señor." Reyna chuckled as she purchased her two black plantains and waved as she headed back into the sunshine.

As Reyna crossed Columbia Road to head south on 18th street, she turned toward a car blaring loud Latin beats. She glared at the car as she stepped into the street and thought, "I know this fool is going to stop at this red light in broad daylight." The fact that he didn't seem aware until it was too late caught Reyna in the midst of stepping back, but she was too slow. Everything seemed to move in a sluggish motion. As the car lurched to brake at the last minute, the fender clipped her left leg; Reyna fell onto the hood of the car, slid off with a bounce and went sprawling across the crosswalk and partially in the flow of traffic on 18th street. It was by the grace of God that cars going north only mashed her bag of plantains and missed her body.

"Ayyy...Dios Mio!" a woman in the gathering crowd called out.

The driver who stumbled out of the car seemed barely old enough to drive. "Hey, lady, you okay? Can you hear me?" He leaned over and peered into Reyna's face. "Jesus, lady, please don't be dead."

Reyna felt the back of her head throbbing where it must have bounced when she fell. Slowly, she opened her eyes to the myriad of blurred faces surrounding her. She heard a police officer make her way into the crowd, while her partner dispersed the crowd and redirected traffic around the incident.

"Miss, can you hear me?"

"Yes," Reyna managed to groan out.

"We have called an ambulance, but do you think you can move at all? Maybe we can get you to the sidewalk?"

Reyna's life saving instincts kicked in. She knew the safest way to move was to turn onto her side. If that was too painful, then she was hurt more than she thought. Slowly, Reyna turned to her side and eased herself upright. Feeling dizzy, she stopped and took a breath as she tried to look around to identify her surroundings. She was relieved to see that she was not lying in any blood. After several painful minutes she was able to stand with the assistance of the female officer who walked her to the sidewalk where a few spectators moved off the available stone benches. Reyna noticed the male officer talking to the driver of the car, who, thankfully, turned his blasting car stereo off.

Reyna gave her information to the female officer. An incident report was written up including the driver's information and statement, and a copy was given to Reyna as they took her away in the ambulance.

Rondel, Mrs. Seaton, and Mr. Seaton were in the Hospital Center's visitor waiting area when the doctor released Reyna a few hours later under strict orders to stay with someone who could monitor her around the clock for 48 hours. She had suffered a sprained wrist, bruised ribs, and a few other minor cuts and bruises. Because Reyna's head hit the pavement the doctor assumed treatment for a mild concussion. Head injuries were not to be taken lightly.

"Well, Ma, I guess I'll be coming over for dinner after all." Reyna said, in an attempt to lighten the mood as her parents and big brother looked on, panic-stricken. She could only imagine what she looked like with bandages wrapped around her hands and head and her clothing dirty and torn.

***

"Li'l Sis, when Ma told me everything that happened last night, I thought you had gone and tossed yourself in front of traffic, and we know that clown was not worth it. I know you saw this coming, anyway. Antoine never had any backbone. I didn't want to say anything while y'all were together, but he was such a punk. He only did whatever you told him to do. Did he ever make any decisions on his own?"

Reyna held her tongue and just thanked the heavens that Rita was away at a conference this fateful weekend. Luckily, she was only subjected to the phone version of her sister's incessant "elder's wisdom". If she wasn't used to her sister's harsh criticisms, Reyna would have gone stark raving mad. Rita didn't want to say anything while she and Antoine were together? The only time Rita didn't criticize was when Reyna didn't talk to her.

"What was that you said, Ma?" Reyna called away from the phone. "It's time for my medicine? Oh, okay. I'll be right down. Sorry 'bout that, Rita, but I need to get off the phone now. Thanks for calling to check on me."

"You know I was going to check on my li'l sis!" Rita gushed.

Reyna shook her head. Her sister really meant well. Rita simply didn't have filters to help control her tongue.

Mrs. Seaton was at the dining room table writing out her bills when Reyna walked down stairs. "Tha's a shame you tellin' them tales to get your sister off the phone." Mrs. Seaton chuckled. "There's a couple of boiled eggs on the stove and cantaloupe slices in the Frigidaire. You probably don't have much of an appetite, but you need to eat something. You want some toast?"

"Nah, I'll get something in a minute. It wasn't a complete tale that I told Rita. I do need some medicine for this headache she gave me. Ma, who does that girl take after? You all sure you didn't find her on the doorstep?" Reyna sat across from her mother with a tall glass of water and popped a couple of the prescribed painkillers.

"You are all sweet children in your own different ways." Mrs. Seaton always defended her babies. She glanced up at Reyna. "How you feeling 'bout Antoine? You really liked him didn't you?"

"Yea." Reyna sighed, "I just feel tired, Ma. And now my head is throbbing to match the ache in my heart. Don't worry, I wasn't throwing myself in front of traffic like Rita thinks."

Reyna looked up to find Mrs. Seaton studying her. "Baby girl...promise me you'll take better care of yourself. Sometimes we don't realize when we're throwing ourselves in front of moving traffic. Our subconscious takes over, and we are less careful and not so alert. Just be aware of what you're saying to yourself at all times, as much as possible. I don't think you intended to get hit yesterday, but I do think that your mind was on other things."

Reyna took another sip of her water and wished it were something stronger. She always prided herself on being self-aware so it pained her to be caught off guard and corrected by her parents when she felt she had outgrown that need.

"Did you and Daddy talk about that at the hospital?"

"Even though me and your daddy ain't together, there are many things we don't need to say to each other aloud. We were young, too, ya know. I know you *young'uns*, as y'all say it, like to think you're the only one struggling through these heartaches and such. Heck, we still alive and get our feathers ruffled by a passing breeze every so often. Just know that we love you dearly. No matter how often you take that boy back into your life, it don't make you a bad person to have needs."

Reyna's eyes widened.

Her mother raised her hand before Reyna could open her mouth.

"I know you don't think you will now, because your feelings are smartin'. But, life don't always work according to our plans. Remember, Baby, if you wanna hear God laugh, tell Him your plans."

All Reyna could do was shake her head and finish her water.

***

Six months had passed. Reyna's physical wounds had healed completely. Emotionally, she was still recovering. Reyna was proud that she had not succumbed to calling on Antoine as her mother predicted. She was especially proud because dating in Washington, D.C. in the early nineties was riddled with challenges, the largest being the ratio of Black women to Black men--which was somewhere in the range of eight females to every male. Reyna did not always believe statistics and knew they could be skewed, but the cavalier behavior of men indicated that this much-promoted statistic could be true. Reyna realized that the noticeable increase in the bisexual and homosexual Black men added to the dating challenge. She decided to focus on her own self-improvement...no matter how frustrated she became. Thanks to Reyna's carnal desires, her workouts rose in frequency and became more vigorous.

One crisp autumn Saturday morning in November, Reyna began sorting her laundry as she did every two weeks. She wondered how she missed his blue button-down shirt and navy blue slacks before. *Maybe*, Reyna sighed as she thought, *the floor at the back of my closet isn't someplace I go as often as I should.* She shook the dust off of them then folded them neatly, disappointed that there was a hint of his cologne and body odor still in them. She resisted the temptation to bury her face and inhale deeply. *He will have to foot his own cleaning bill this time*, she smirked as she walked to her foyer closet and pulled out the box of Antoine's items she had found interspersed throughout her home. Reyna often toyed with the idea of burning the copier-paper box filled with his books, jewelry, toothbrush and--now--clothing in effigy, but her Christian upbringing would not let her.

Reyna looked through her student directory and called his brother, Corey Davis.

"Good morning, Mr. Davis, I apologize for calling on your day off."

Corey chuckled, "Reyna, you don't need to address me so formally. We're still friends regardless of the bad decision of my brother. To what do we owe the pleasure of this call?"

"Thanks, Corey." Reyna sighed with some relief. "This is just very awkward for me. I was cleaning up and found that I still have some items that belong to Antoine, but I don't want to call him. Is it okay if I drop them off at your place?"

"Oh, uh...sure. I understand. Yeah, bring the items by at your convenience. If we're not here, the housekeeper will be here."

"Great. I'll bring them by at around six this evening."

"And, Reyna..."

Reyna held her breath, "Yes?"

"I really do apologize for my brother. He's always been very spoiled. I had hoped that spending time with you would help him mature a bit. I'm really sorry I ever introduced you."

Me, too, Reyna thought but answered, "I appreciate the fact that you thought I could be such an influence...Okay, then. Let me finish up in here, then I'll bring these items to you."

Corey said softly, "Take care of yourself, Reyna."

***

Reyna pulled up in front of the beautiful, slate blue-grey Victorian styled home in the Brookland neighborhood. She arrived a couple of hours earlier than she told Corey because Reyna wanted this box and him out of her home, life and--eventually, she hoped--heart. Reyna put her head on the steering wheel of her Subaru. "Just take the box to the door, ring the bell, and smile at whoever answers," said Reyna as she gave herself a little pep talk. She wondered why her stomach was churning and her palms were sweating. "You can do this." Taking a deep breath, she exited the car and walked behind it to open her trunk. She froze when she heard his voice from the front walk.

"A'ight, man. Thanks again. I'll have this back to you by next week!"

Reyna wanted to climb into the trunk and close it. Too late--he saw her.

Walking toward her, Antoine smiled as he slid his eyes over her, "Hey, Reyna. What are you doing here?"

Try not to pass slam out, Reyna thought as she gathered herself, prayed he didn't notice her shaking hands and answered. "Actually, I was bringing your belongings to your brother."

Corey jogged from the house to join them on the sidewalk. Looking fairly embarrassed, he managed, "Hey, Reyna...uh...we weren't expecting you until later."

Antoine looked from one to the other quizzically, "You didn't tell me Reyna was coming over."

"I apologize, Corey. I just finished up sooner than I'd planned." Reyna turned to Antoine with the box she'd lifted from the trunk. "I called Corey because I had hoped I could avoid seeing you...but so much for that. So, Antoine, here are the last of the things you left at my place."

"Oh... thanks. It's good to see you again."

"Thanks." Reyna bit her tongue and did not add that she wished she could say the same. "Corey, I hope I didn't impose on you."

"Not at all. I'm sorry..." Corey's face looked confused and mournful at the same time. Reyna felt bad that he seemed caught in the middle. Still, a part of her was pissed at him, too. He knew his brother was a hound. Reyna reminded herself to let it go.

"Well, I've taken up enough of your time, and I've got some work to prepare for next week's classes. Tell Lena and the family hello for me, please. You both have a good evening."

They stood on the sidewalk watching her as Reyna got into her car and drove away. When she was a block away, Reyna screamed at the top of her lungs. She wanted to get out and run some of her nervous energy off. "DAMMIT! Why do men look better after your relationship with them ends?! Well, at least I didn't cry or get emotional. I am thankful for that."

Of course, as soon as she arrived home, Reyna called her girl, Sydnee, and ranted about Antoine.

"Sydnee, do you know that *'bama* had the nerve to grin at me and look me up and down like there is ANY possibility that he was going to get with me again! UGH! Brothers are so *dayum* arrogant sometimes!"

"Yeah, the confidence is a double-edged sword. But, you can't be mad at him for looking you over like the last slice o' pie. You *have* been hitting the gym pretty hard lately."

Reyna had to laugh along with Sydnee, "You're right. If I do say so myself, Body IS kinda tight these days!"

"You can admit it to me; you were glad he ran into you."

"Girll, I was too nervous at the time, but now--yeah, it was good to see his mouth watering. Ha haaaa!"

Once that topic was exhausted, Sydnee hit Reyna with surprising news.

"Rey, I know I should tell you this in person, but I'm about to burst now. Before he left a few hours ago, Bruce asked me to move to New York with him."

Reyna was stunned. She just got over her boyfriend breaking up with her, and she felt now that her best friend was dumping her.

"Rey, you there?"

"Wow...Wow. I don't know what else to say."

"I know. I was surprised, too. I still don't really believe that I'm seriously considering it. I mean, I like Bruce, and I love our sex life; and I'm not flighty enough to believe that will be enough for a relationship. I think he really wants to see if we can have a real relationship. I just don't really know what to do, Rey."

"Did he say he wants to marry you? I'm confused."

"Girl, no more confused than I am. I don't know if he wants marriage or if he's afraid to mention it because I'm always so vocal about no strings!"

"I thought you said you communicate openly with your men. You shouldn't be confused like I usually am."

Sydnee laughed on the other end of the phone. "That's what I've been telling myself since Bruce asked me to go with him. I don't even know if he really meant to ask me or if it was just in the glow of the aftermath. You know everything sounds like a great idea after great sex. I did have the sense to tell him we'd talk more about it tomorrow, and I'll make sure we talk before we undress. But even now, I'm wondering if I hurt his feelings by saying let's talk about it tomorrow. Reyna Girllll, men can be some of the hardest creatures to figure out!"

"You preachin' to the choir, now! I thought you were the one who had this all figured out!" Reyna was surprised she could really laugh, when she just wanted to start bawling all over again.

"I don't know if I'm more excited that Bruce wants me to join him...or that I may actually get the chance to live in The Big Apple. I do love that city."

"Slow down, Sistah Syd. You know when you move, it won't be endless shoe shopping like when we visit." Reyna chuckled and almost got into the spirit of Sydnee's excitement.

"Well, when *you* visit, I'll take the time for shoe shopping!" Sydnee giggled.

Reyna couldn't believe that Sydnee was giggling like a teenager. This was Hurricane Sydnee who always saved the day for everyone else. "What about your job?"

"As a nurse, I can find a job anywhere. With all the fools in New York, I know they need nurses big time!"

"Well, you're right about that. Dang, I'm gonna miss you, Syd."

Sydnee chuckled with compassion, "It's not like I'm going to the west coast. New York's only a four-hour drive, a blink of a flight and a phone call away. Heck, I've had booty calls come that far."

"There *you* go...and Bruce is going to put a stop to your booty calls, now."

"Yea, well...I'll give this cowboy all the rope he needs. I just hope he knows what to do with me once he's got me all to himself."

"Please don't get that man to New York and send him into cardiac arrest. Uhhooo, 'scuz me for yawnin' in your ear!"

"Dang, Rey. It's not even ten yet--and on a Saturday at that." Sydnee laughed.

"I guess getting up early this morning is taking its toll. I can't hang like I used to." Reyna admitted.

"You goin' to church tomorrow?"

"Yea, our choir sings at the seven-thirty service so I need to get in the bed now, anyway. You coming through?"

"If I do, it won't be at the seven-thirty service."

"Well, I'll put in a prayer for ya."

"Please do. You know I need all the prayers I can get, Rey."

"Alrighty, Supah Soul Sistah--I'll holla wit' ya tomorrow."

Reyna undressed and prepared for bed. Her phone rang as she was wrapping her hair up for the night. Assuming Sydnee had forgotten some salt to rub into her wounds, Reyna picked up the phone with a witty, "Girl, don't tell me he came back to ask you to marry him?"

A male voice responded, "Rey?"

She became stock-still as she recognized his voice.

"Rey, you there?"

Reyna whispered, "Yes."

"Are you busy? Can I talk to you for a minute?"

"About what?" Reyna's voice chilled as she lowered herself to the edge of her bed.

Antoine chuckled nervously, "Uh, I need to see you."

"*What*? Why? Everything you left was in that box."

"I know it was, sweetness. It's not that. It's, uh...damn, I'll understand if you say no, but it was just so good to see you earlier. It hit me how much I miss you, and I just want to see you for a few minutes." The phone began the clicking noise that starts after several minutes into a call, indicating that the call was coming from her entry system.

"You had the nerve to come *here*?!" Reyna practically screeched.

"Look, will you buzz me in so we can talk? I just want ..."

Reyna slammed the phone down ... and buzzed him in.

Fast Food Conversation

when we talk about
flirtations and betrayal
        I always ask
why some men
stray
when they have
the perfect woman
waiting for them
at home
        I always wonder
why would he choose
a big mac
over a filet mignon?
        These questions never quit
his answer
        What he actually said to me
was that sometimes
a man
just feels like
        eating
          fast food

Saadia Ali Aschemann

Lies About Love

love is never enough
it doesn't pay the rent
or make the world go 'round
it hardly conquers all
love is clearly not blind
and rarely patient
seldom is it kind
and love is
not even close
to being a
many splendored thing
it is an optimist's ideal
a pessimist's smug lore
love lives
despite the lies
it tells

Saadia Ali Aschemann

Dedication

To my son, my nephews, my brothers, my fathers, Jena 6, Genarlow Wilson, and all the young men out there who are striving to be somebody...don't get caught up in the game. To the men and women who are raising their sons, and mentoring to the community. I commend you!!

Smoke

By Diane Dorce'

    It was Saturday night in probably one of the last places I wanted to be. In fact I could think of three or four different locations and better company than Smoke's Bar and Grill. But I was trying to stop a murder and, next to Superman, Smoke was the only man I knew who could stop a bullet.

    "Jack okay with you?" Smoke hollered from the bar.

    "Yeah," I said, and watched while he poured two full- to-the rim shots of Jack Daniels. My mouth watered at the sight. Although I was not normally a drinker, on a day like today, I needed it more than I needed a woman or food (which was usually what I needed just about everyday, but not today). Today started off rocky at best and gradually descended into premature hell, and with the gatekeeper by my side, I was sure I'd be meeting up with Satan any moment. "Hey, you alright?" I asked him, but I don't know why; the boy hadn't said two words to me since I picked him up at Georgia Correctional Institute--which, to me, sounded like a big, fancy name for *jail*.

    "It stinks in here."

    Damn, he could talk...but he was right. That mixture of smoked meat, liquor and some other gaseous substance I couldn't quite distinguish--but smelled a lot like funk--wasn't exactly the kind of thing you wanted to breathe in on the regular.

"It will pass." That's the one thing I knew for sure; sit here long enough and you become used to it.

Smoke dragged himself from around the bar, pulling on his wood leg, like he had bricks tied to it. It didn't seem like that long ago Smoke was jumping five foot fences in one sweeping motion, peg leg and all. Old Father Time had other plans though. Easily pushing sixty, Smoke moved like a man twenty years older--tired and at the end of his rope. After all these years, he still looked the same, wore the same part down the middle of his head like back in the day and dyed it twice a month so he wouldn't go entirely white. I always thought it was foolish for a man to dye his hair, but I probably wouldn't recognize Smoke without that black hair dye, let alone the part.

Smoke poured drinks, grilled ribs and fried fish from five to midnight on Saturday and every other Sunday. He had a diverse clientele consisting of pimps, players, drug dealers, prostitutes, politicians and cops (but not all on the same night). Smoke's place was just above an average shack with four wobbly tables, twelve chairs, a jukebox and one bar stool that Bebe, Smoke's step-sister, occupied much of the time. What the place lacked in décor, it made up in history and some of the best times I had ever experienced. Let Smoke tell it, some of the baddest dudes that ever ran the streets of Atlanta damn near lived in Smoke's. It was where we hung out, done deals--even beat a few heads if need be. Bottom line, the joint was a staple around these parts, as much as Ebenezer Baptist Church, Auburn Avenue and the Martin Luther King Center. Just like the others, it had served its purpose over time.

Smoke's eyes were still fierce and capable of a champion stare-down that would rival Mike Tyson's. He never took his eyes off the boy. "You got a name?" he asked, placing the two shot glasses on the table and taking a seat across from me and beside the boy.

The boy seemed annoyed, like he wasn't meant to answer to anyone, shrugging his shoulders and shifting in his seat. He struck that obvious *bad boy* pose with his head leaning to the side and his arms folded in front of him, then barked out his name "Mad Dog," he said.

Smoke downed his shot, coughed a little, and then shook his head. "That's a muthafucking shame. Someone named this boy some shit like "Mad Dog!" He looked over at me. "What you think, Willie?"

I could feel the hairs raise up on the back of my neck. This wasn't going exactly as I planned--in fact, worse. I spoke up, trying to ease the tension, although I didn't know what good it would do. "Boy's name is Tyrell. I seen it on his release papers." It was my job to get him and bring him here. I knew more about him than I wanted to know. I knew all about his arrest, how he botched up a simple robbery, and got caught holding the goodies. He grew up poor and--mosttimes--on the street. His mama was a crackhead and his daddy ran off and left before the semen dried. Yeah, I knew more about Tyrell then he knew about himself, because...he was just a mirror image of me.

Tyrell sat with his head between his legs, not bothering to address either of us. I guess he didn't really know what to say.

"Willie, go'on around the bar and grab us the bottle. Looks like it's gonna be a long night."

"The bottle" Smoke referred to was empty, but resting comfortably on a shelf below the bar were rows and rows of liquor. Twenty or more so jam jars, filled with liquor and labeled specifically with its brand--Stolichnaya, Grey Goose, Hennessy, Martell and Remy, to name a few. Smoke never carried the original bottles, always discarded them or simply didn't bring them into the establishment. This way, he had to deal with less break-ins and theft, and, with a little paper and lot of greasing hands, he operated without a liquor license because this really wasn't a bar. Well, it was our bar, and Monday through Sunday--sunup to sundown, we drank, sucked on rib tips, shot bones, and talked shit.

Bebe, Smoke's sister, sat in the corner nodding her head to an imaginary beat. She wore close to nothing, and the sight of her sagging breasts was enough to make you sick. She looked like life or some man had sucked the wind out of her, but, in reality, it was heroin that did her in. Bebe was in a world of her own--had been for many years. That song she was singing was her life playing over and over again. I felt sorry for her but didn't let my eyes linger too long. I brought the bottle to the table and poured us two more drinks. Smoke downed his drink in one gulp. I sipped mine.

"So, Willie, what's up? I thought you was still shakin' them fools on Peachtree?"

"Naw man, I'm chillin'," I said looking over at Tyrell, who looked down at the floor to keep from looking at Bebe. "He looking for a gig, man. Thought you could hook him up with something."

Smoke eyed the young man sitting at the table, his head hanging between his legs. Willie could tell he wasn't pleased with what he saw. The boy couldn't be no older than fifteen, sixteen at most, skinny as a rail, hair going every which way, and his clothes were dirty and stained. Smoke shook his head, grunted, and then sucked at his teeth. Something he always did when he wasn't pleased. "Man what I'm gonna do with this rugrat?" He sucked his teeth again. "The boy is weak."

Tyrell jumped up from his seat, almost knocking it to the ground. "I ain't weak, motherfucker!" he shouted in Smoke's direction.

The commotion snapped Bebe out of her daze and she shouted at no one in particular, "Motherfucker, I'll cut ya!" wielding an imaginary knife, "I'll cut ya."

I reached for the boy, pulling him by the back of his shirt, "Sit down."

Smoke had already pulled his piece. If he wanted to kill him, the boy would have been dead before his chair hit the floor. The boy saw what I saw, but he was stubborn and mean. He did what he was told and finally took a seat...but only after I had practically snatched a hole in his t-shirt and nearly choked him to death. I guess the name "Mad Dog" fit.

"Smoke, its cool, man," I said. "He fresh, you know-- how we used to be." Smoke was almost fifteen years older than I was, but we ran the streets something fierce back in the day. He was that crazy, cool type of nigga down for anything and everything, the dude you counted on when things got rough.

Bebe was still howling at the moon when Smoke banged his leg against the wooden table, garnering her attention as well as everyone else's. "Bebe! Chill! It's alright," he said a little softer. "Ain't that right, boy?" Smoke pulled out his wallet and peeled off a couple of fifties, handing them over to me. "First things first, the boy needs some clothes. He can't be hanging around here like that. Buy him some things. I'll catch up with you later at the house."

***

I ain't never liked shopping much. I copped most of my clothes from shelters and second-hand stores; that's why I found it a pain to be shopping like a woman to clothe some boy's ass.

"How much you got there?" Tyrell asked, leaning in his seat and reaching for my wallet lying on top of the dashboard.

I grabbed the wallet and stuffed it on the seat beside me. "Boy, I know you better watch them hands 'fore you lose 'em."

Tyrell snatched his hands back and laughed like something was funny. I didn't really know what to make of the boy. Sometimes he acted like he had some sense, and sometimes he was more ignorant than Funky Perry down on Peachtree. Funky Perry preached every day of the week, right in front of the Underground. Most times he was drunk, but even when he was sober he didn't make much sense, least not to normal folks. If you listened to Funky Perry tell it, everybody was going to hell--the Christians, Jews, Muslims, Jehovah Witnesses. He didn't have a kind word for anybody except Rufus. Rufus and his kind would rule the earth and inherit the Kingdom of Heaven. Funny thing, Rufus always barked at that exact moment as if he understood everything Funky Perry said and was in agreement. Yep, Funky Perry had Rufus as his anointed savior, while Tyrell worshipped money and lots of it.

"Yo, you pretty quick for an old dude. That shit was funny. Yo' eyes all bucking, like them dudes in the old movies--yassa, yassa," he mocked, laughing.

I laughed, too! Shit, it was funny. The boy had jokes, and that was good. You had to learn how to laugh some times, and I ain't never been afraid of laughing at myself. "Yeah, well, fuck you, okay."

"Alright, G, it's cool. Really, my bad. Y'all done went and got me out of that hellhole, and you trying to do something here with buying me clothes and shit. It's all good, but why?"

"I don't know, my man. You have to ask Smoke about it. It's his call. I'm just the messenger and, sometime chauffeur."

"Oh, so he like Mr. Big or something?"

"Yeah, something like that."

***

I spent all day watching that boy...shop like a girl, until I couldn't take it no more. How much looking can you do? You find what you want and you buy it. Well, I knew with him it was much more than that; he had been incarcerated for so long, just the thought of being free made him a little bit crazy--and me too!

Tyrell picked up a couple of large t-shirts, some baggy pants and one dress shirt I encouraged him to buy-- despite his obvious objections. I knew a man had to have some dress clothes. If only for weddings, funerals, job interviews or court, dress clothes were an essential. He laughed when I told him that like I was telling another joke or something, but I was serious. Serious as a heart attack.

"I ain't gonna wear this!" He pointed to the dress shirt and dress pants I paid for.

"You never know--"

"Yeah, I do know. This is lame. A nigga like me don't be wearing no tie and shit!"

"A nigga like you needs to in the appropriate time. Why you always calling yourself 'a nigga' anyway? Don't you understand the negative connotations associated with that word? You ain't no 'nigga'! You a young black boy *trying to be a man.* Stop using that to define yourself. You can be better than that, Tyrell."

"Yeah? Like what?" He gave me an inquisitive look. "Like you? Somebody's lackey, chauffeur...like Mr. Big, some old-school big dog living in a shack. That's whack, homey. Im'a be bigger than that. Shit...I know all about these streets...and I got game."

I shook my head at his audacity to demean me or Smoke. That's what's wrong with young folks today, they just don't understand. Game, my *ass*.

"You ain't got shit, young man. All you got is what we give you...Smoke and I."

He looked at me strange, kind of sad-like. But, it was the truth, and I know the truth hurts some times--but it was the only thing to set you free. I just hoped he heard me.

***

Now about that murder I was trying to stop: The boy had got himself into more trouble than he had imagined. The only reason he was released early was because he turned state's evidence on one bad dude who went by the name of Juan G. Juan G was a gang leader, drug runner, and once-convicted murderer. Unbelievably, even with Tyrell's confession, he was still free and walking the streets. Tyrell didn't know that, but Smoke and I knew; and it was up to us to protect him as best we could until something could be worked out. Juan G aka Juan Thomas was in his early twenties, a young buck with a lot of street credibility. He ran his game out of his grandma's house on the Westside, and he had every street and neighborhood between West End and Bankhead on lock.

How Tyrell got mixed up with him, I don't know--but he
did...and this was the result. We had a plan, Smoke and I-
-we would meet with Juan and make a deal. We still had
one up on him; he didn't know Tyrell was out, and he didn't
know that Tyrell was the one that fingered him. But, we
also knew that our time was short because--for little or
nothing, the streets talked, and it wouldn't take but a day
or two until they revealed all.

"Where we going now?" Tyrell interrupted.

"Back to Smoke's place."

"Why? I thought I might check out some of my
homies...go see my ma."

He referred to his grandma as "ma", because his
real mother been out of the picture for years.

"You can see your grandma later--not today."

"How about my homies, man? I ain't kicked it with
them in over a year. I miss them niggas."

I looked at him.

"I mean, I miss *them*."

"Alright then, that's better. Look, son, just do what
I say, and you will live to see them another day."

"Why you say it like that? Like I ain't gonna live?"

I didn't know if he was asking me to be funny or if
he was just that stupid. I pulled the car over, into a
shopping center because what I had to say, I had to say it
looking him directly in the eye.

"Tyrell, you know why you were released?"

"Yeah, I served my time."

"No, you were given three years; you served a year
and a half. Now, I'm gonna ask you again. *Do you know
why you were released early?*"

"No," he hunched his shoulders, "you tell me."

"Did you tell anyone who orchestrated the robbery?
Did you give them a name?"

"Hell *naw*! I didn't tell them shit. I ain't no snitch."

"You didn't tell them anything about Juan G?"

"What?"

His eyes got big and he looked like the wind had been knocked out of him. The name scared him--as well it should have.

"Juan G, aka Juan Thomas. Did you mention him to the cops or legal?"

"No, I don't know nothing about no Juan G, man." He looked out the window.

"Well looka here, son, I'm just keeping it real. The word is out that you fingered Juan, and, if that's true or if he only believes it to be true, he's coming after you. So I hope for your sake that's its not, but, to tell you the truth, it ain't looking good either way."

He didn't say a word. Kept his face turned towards the window, but I noticed the slight movement of his hand brushing against his cheek. And, I saw his chest rise and fall heavily at first, then rapidly. I wanted to reach out to him, to let him know that we weren't gonna let anything happen to him, that we were indeed the "original g's" and that we--Smoke and I were--willing to lay down our lives for him. I wanted to tell him all of that, but I told him nothing. That's when he opened up and told all.

***

"It didn't go down like that," he halfway muttered, face still turned away from me. I guess he didn't want me to see the tears, but I know choked-up when I see it.

"What happened?"

"Just some bullshit. We weren't even thinking about robbing nobody, especially no lame grocery store, not until...." He paused. "Not until he rolled up."

"Juan G?"

"Yeah, that's what he liked to call himself. Every nigga on the street was jockeying for him. Me--I didn't know shit about him and didn't care."

"So why you get involved?"

"The streets are like that. You don't want somebody thinking you soft. Thinking you ain't got the balls to handle some small shit. I wasn't into it, but I did it. That's just how it is."

I knew more than what he told me. I knew all about the streets and what they offered, the games they played on young minds like Tyrell. I could tell him a shitload of stories, but I didn't. I just sat back and listened.

"Juan G says if we brought back the loot, we was in for life. Anything we wanted was delivered like that," he snapped his fingers. "I respected that nigga. I did, and all I wanted to do was get it done, do it fast and get out, but it didn't happen that way."

Tyrell fidgeted in his seat and twisted another strand of hair.

"So, you got left holding the bag?"

"I got left. Period."

I waited for him to tell me more, but he didn't. He went back into his shell, turned towards the window. I didn't know the whole story, but I was able to piece together a scenario based upon the police reports Smoke was able to gather and a short write-up in the *Journal-Constitution*.

It was a small time robbery, a local convenience store just around the corner from his grandma's. Him and two others went in--scarves over their faces--two of them brandishing guns; Juan G was believed to be the lead man. Everything was going according to plan until the store owner returned through the back door and surprised them with a 20-gauge shotgun, injuring one of the youths. The lead man returned fire, killing the owner. Tyrell was identified as one of three. The other boy died from his injuries so Tyrell's the only one who knows the truth and the only one who could tie Juan G to the crime. It was a heavy load to carry for any man. For a boy of fifteen, it had to be devastating. I thought back to my childhood, my teen years. Sure, there was violence--we had gangs-- but the community supported each other; we were all we had. We didn't rob and steal from each other like they do today. I shook my head, not knowing what else to say... or really do, for that matter. I just knew that I wanted to help... help this one boy.

"You hungry?" I asked.

"Yeah."

"Then, let's eat. Smoke should be just about finished with those ribs."

***

The drive back to Smoke's place was, for the most part, a quiet one. I let the boy vacation with his thoughts and contend with his demons just a little longer before I decided to engage him in more conversation. There was something to be said about silence; not everyone knew or appreciated it the way I did. *A conscious man listens and hears.* When I first heard that, I thought, *That's silly; if you listening, then you are also hearing--what's the difference?* But, there is a difference; everyone hearing, ain't listening. Like when Tyrell wants to play that hip-hop music on my radio--I hear it, but I ain't *listening*.

Smoke's place was jumping. There were cars lined up and down Moreland Avenue, some even double-parked. Out back, large funnels of smoke wisped through the air carrying with them the smell of ribs, chicken, and grilled burgers. There were countless times I had visited Smoke, and he was out back grilling while folks inside and out were playing cards, shooting dice, dancing and drinking from sunup to sundown.

"Looks like plenty to eat here. Go'on over there and grab you a plate of something."

I didn't have to tell Tyrell twice; he was out the car and up the walk before I could blink an eye.

"What up Dude?" Smoke hollered. "He lookin' a whole lot better than when he left, *a whole lot* better."

"Yeah... now, all he needs is a haircut."

Smoke laughed hard and closed the lid on the grill. "Come on, Willie. You not gonna believe who came by!"

He grabbed me around the shoulders and shuffled me in through the door, and I was more than surprised to see some of our old partners from back in the day, a few of the policemen who locked me up time and time again when I didn't know any better and my old lady, Desiree.

"You remember Desi, don't you?" Smoke said laughing too loud.

Desiree was still the picture of cuteness, even if she had put on a little extra weight. She had always been thick and wide at the bottom; now it seemed she just filled in the middle. I was still glad to see her... real glad. I had one word for Desiree, *Juicy*!

"Desiree Mitchell, how you doing?"

"Fine, Willie" smacking her orange glazed lips. "Smoke told me you were back around. I ain't seen you for a minute though. You wanna buy me a drink?"

"Yeah, Hun, sure."

Smoke stepped in, "Naw, Willie, yo money ain't no good here--it's on the house. Yo! Mad Dog!" he said laughing, "Pour this here lady a Jack Daniels on the rocks."

Tyrell removed the last of a rib bone from his mouth and looked real funny at the both of us. I nodded at him, hoping he wouldn't put up no fuss and start living up to his nickname...and he surprised me by doing exactly what I wanted.

"Yessir," he said. "One Jack Daniels coming up."

Smoke looked at me and smiled. "I'm starting to like that boy."

"Yeah--me too...me, too."

With the promise of free drinks all night I pretty much had Miss Desiree eating out of my hands, and, though I was interested in a little one-on-one, I still had some business to take care of with Smoke. We headed to the back room to hash out a plan.

"Bring the bottle, Willie. This may take all night."

I did as he said and sat the bottle of Jack on the small, rickety table. This was what Smoke called his "office". It was a little more than a broom closet, with a desk, a table, a small metal file cabinet and a lamp that had seen its last days.

Smoke lit up a cigar and puffed hard. "So I made contact with that dude, Juan and we supposed to meet later on tonight."

My ears perked up after hearing his name. "What he say?"

"He ain't say shit. I did the talking. Told him I know what he was in to--that if he wanted to avoid a whole lot of heat, we needed to meet--that's it."

"Okay, so where y'all meeting?"

Smoke looked at me crazy-like, like I asked something stupid.

"Here. He is coming here tonight." He took another drag, letting the smoke drift out of his mouth and nose and into the air...and watched it as it floated up to the ceiling. "I had to cut back on these. Doctor says smoking is no good for my lungs, but fuck'em."

I laughed.

"You know what I mean. They always trying to tell us what's good for us, but them doctors be smoking and drinking too, all the time. You want one?" he asked.

"Naw, man, I'm straight. That shit be burning my insides." I didn't want to mention to him that it was also burning my eyes or the prospect of secondhand smoke. He didn't want to hear that shit. "What we gonna do about the boy?"

"After tonight, everything will be cool. He can go back to living with his grandma, go to school, work--you know. Shit, the nigga will have his life back."
It all sounded so good...like some fairytale shit. I knew that and I would bet a dollar that Smoke knew that, too.

"Oh--and so, that's it. You not gonna tell the boy the truth?"

He puffed again and shook his head. "Don't see no reason why I have to. What went down years ago is over and done with. He don't need to know about that. I didn't have a chance before, so I'm giving him a chance now. I'm sacrificing everything on him doing the right thing...that's what a father should do."

"So you not gonna tell him you his daddy?"

I knew I was stepping way out of line--it was not my call at all to be discussing Smoke's business--but I had come to like Tyrell and I wanted more for him than the streets. He deserved a family, a mother and a father, and, since his mama was gone, he at least deserved his father.

Smoke puffed on his cigar until it was down to nub-sized, and then rubbed the last of it in ashtray. "Some things are better left alone, Willie. That boy don't know me from anybody else. I'd like to keep it that way. We can be friends, maybe...but, if not, I will go to my grave knowing I did what I could for him."

I disagreed big time, but I knew there was no changing Smoke's mind...so I said nothing.

Someone had started up the jukebox and the voice of the late, great Phyllis Hyman graced our ears singing "Somewhere, In My Lifetime." All I could do was sit back and listen. Grooving to the music that was so clear and pure, you would have thought Miss Hyman was in the next room. Even when I couldn't hear the instrumental background, her voice seeped through every nook, cranny and floor board to reach us.

"Dayum, it sounds like Phyllis is in the next room" I said.

Smoke laughed. "Nigga, that ain't no Phyllis--that's *Bebe*."

I jumped up from my chair and damn near tripped over my feet getting back to the bar. I had to see it for myself, yet when I set my eyes on Bebe, I saw her entirely different. Nothing physical had changed about her--in the same corner, on the same stool, and the same disheveled appearance--except for that angelic, soulful voice that had everyone in the room in a trance. I felt something come over me like grief mixed with joy, a thunderstorm of emotions I didn't quite understand and tried to swallow away.

Smoke walked up. "Didn't know she could blow like that, did ya?"

The best I could do was shake my head.

"I know--she gets to you." He pointed towards his chest. "Gets you here--down deep--me, too! I wish she would sing like that all the time, but it comes and goes-- never planned...just when she gets to feeling like she wants to."

Bebe sang one last verse then leaned forward with her eyes closed. People in the bar didn't know whether to clap or not. We all just sat there waiting for something or someone to cut into the silence, to draw us back into the real world. Smoke would be our savior

"Ah! I need me another drink. Bartender!" he yelled at Tyrell, "Fix me up a double."

***

By eight-o-clock, the party was in full swing. Jukebox was blowing up some old school bands like Brass Construction, SOS Band and Parliament Funkadelic. Heck, I even saw young Terrell bobbing his head to the beat and enjoying himself. Although I didn't really think it was the proper place for the boy to be hanging out, with all the drinking, smoking and gambling going on Smoke didn't think twice about him being there and even took the opportunity to introduce Tyrell to some of Atlanta's elite.

"I want you to meet my new assistant manager-in-training." That's how he introduced him, and Tyrell seemed to be enjoying the attention.

I was on my second game of spades when Juan G arrived with his posse. Everyone froze like a scene out of a movie when the bad guy enters the bar with his guns drawn, always surrounded by knuckleheads.

"Well, well, well, ain't this a pretty little piece you got here, Smoke? I didn't know you had it going on like this?" Juan G said glancing over the clientele.

I always thought it was a bad idea bringing him here, but Smoke thought different. On this particular night, we had two attorneys, the City Councilman, the Police Chief, and some of Smoke's riding buddies. It was a unique and diverse crowd, but not a one of them was lacking nerves or firepower.

"Juan G, what's up man? Come on back," Smoke said motioning to the back room. "But you gonna have to leave your heat at the door, my man."

Two of Smoke's riding buddies patted Juan G down.

Juan G laughed. "Alright, my man, it's all good," he said as he looked around the room...until his eyes rested on Tyrell.

"I know you. Don't I? Baby T, right? You don't look like no baby no more--guess that little bit of time got you all beefed up. What up, dude? You not gonna show me no love?"

"Fuck you, nigga!" Tyrell barked out.

Juan G's crew jumped into action but was quickly shut down by the riders and a few off-duty policemen.

"Whoa, little man, you got a big mouth for such a little frame. Feeling froggy is you?"

"Look," Smoke interrupted, "We got business in the back. Willie, bring us a bottle. What you drinking, Juan?"

"I don't."

"Well, bring me a bottle, then."

Once Smoke and Juan were out of the room, things sort of returned to normal. The jukebox was turned up again; the card games were back in full swing but I couldn't concentrate on nothing but was taking place in the next room. I also wanted to check on Tyrell because he looked like he was about to attack someone, and this was neither the right place nor time.

"Yo, Tyrell, hand me that bottle of Jack Daniels underneath the cabinet."

He gave it to me, never taking his eyes off of Juan's cronies or the door.

"What's up with you? You need to shut your ass up and let Smoke handle this."

Tyrell was all puffed up like those fish I saw on PBS. One prick, he would have exploded. It was enough to have to face Juan G and his cast of cronies; I damn sure didn't feel like taking this boy down a size.

"Jack," he said slamming the bottle down on the counter.

I took the bottle and headed back to Smoke's office. I knocked twice and entered.

"Willie, my man, sit that down right here," Smoke pointed at the small table.

I did as I was told and proceeded to leave, having no more business in there, when Smoke called.

"Hold up, man, I want you to hear this. Juan here says he got a deal for us. Says he won't lift a finger against Tyrell if we give him half of the profits of the bar and grill. Get this; he's not talking about just tonight, my man--no, he means every week, from now on. Now, where we come from, boy, that's called a *shakedown*, ain't that right, Willie?"

I nodded. Man, oh man...I'm thinking, *This fool had the nerve to come up in here and shakedown Smoke.* I looked from one to the other. Neither one of them was about to give, and I really wasn't liking the vibe at all. Juan G laughed loud.

"Ole dude, that's the terms. You can take it or leave it."

Smoke brought the bottle of Jack crashing down onto the desk in front of him, shattering it to pieces and barely missing Juan G's hand.

"You think you can come into my place and fucking threaten me and my family," he held the broken-edged bottle up to Juan's neck. "You are thinking the wrong thing, son. You put one hand, touch *one hair* of my boy and I will wipe out your entire block--or perhaps I should just put an end to all this shit now, by wiping out your ass."

Juan G said nothing, only smiled and attempted to brush the glass and liquor from his Sean Jean jacket. He raised his hands slowly. "It's cool, Ole G. I mean I deserved that. Family means everything to me, too. I guess we have to work something else out then. It's like this; he needs to disappear--soon. Any witness is no good to me--and everybody knows where he is, so you make him vanish...and I won't have to. Comprende?"

***

Juan G's trial was set to begin in three weeks. According to Smoke, that gave us plenty of time to ship Tyrell safely away. But, for the most part we did nothing but enjoy spending time together, like a real family.

"Uncle Smoke, this shit is boring! I hadn't caught jack!"

Smoke belted out a laugh and turned over the steaks he had grilling. "Be patient, young man; fish don't like to be rushed. I told you that's why fishing is a great sport--it teaches you patience."

"Aunt Bebe, watch your feet. You're gonna get wet" Tyrell said, guiding Bebe away from the edge of the lake.

I watched with added interest noting how, in just a few weeks we had become Tyrell's primary family and he our prodigal son. He even got his hair cut and was expressing interest in returning to school. The one thing he didn't know was he wouldn't be living here. Smoke didn't want to tell him until the last minute...says he didn't want to spoil the mood.

"Hey, Uncle Willie, check this out! I think I got one, Uncle Smoke--the line is moving!" Tyrell screamed.

"Hold the line, son, then reel him in slow. Willie, watch the grill," Smoke hollered then wobbled down the hill to join Tyrell and Bebe.

"Shit! It must be big one."

"Hold on, boy!" Smoke grabbed a hold to the pole, steadying it between himself and Tyrell. "Now turn... slow...slow. Alright--that's it."

Bebe hollered in the background, just as excited. "He got one! He got one!"

"Bebe, shush before you scare him."

"Ahhhh, I got it! Look--*damn* it's big!"

"Grab it! Whew, dog! That's a *bass*. Must weigh about fifteen pounds," Smoke said, tugging at the pole.

Smoke was smiling so hard, I thought his face would split...and I couldn't be happier for him. All his life he wanted children, but never had any, (not that he knew of). He didn't find out about Tyrell until the boy was sentenced--that's when the grandmother came to him for help. Tyrell's mother left him with her mother when the boy was five years old. Smoke had been given a second chance; in a sense we all had.

"Hey, Uncle Willie, check me out. Supreme fisherman!"

***

The rest of the evening was filled with food, drink and talk. I never been much of the "camping out" type, but this was good and peaceful. After eating just about all of the food Smoke had grilled, we sat around the campfire and swapped stories—some old and some new. Smoke and I drank some more of his fine whiskey, while Bebe nursed a warm beer she'd been holding onto since early afternoon. The light of the moon gleamed through the trees, and the crickets harmonized as we took our first steps into becoming a family.

"So Uncle Willie, I ain't trying to diss or nothing, but when you gonna get rid of that Gerri Curl?"

Smoke nearly choked and laughed so hard he cried. "I've been telling him that for years. He don't listen."

"Man, ain't nothing wrong with my hair. I keep it neat. Shit, it ain't never stopped me from picking up no woman."

Tyrell and Smoke couldn't stop laughing.

"Naw, Unc, it's cool."

"Y'all fucking with me" I said between chewings on a toothpick. "For real, though, young man that birds nest you wearing ain't exactly hitting on nothing."

The boy tried to comb his fingers through the mangled mess but stopped.

"Im'a get it cut."

"You are?"

"Yep. So if I get mine cut, will you get yours cut?"

Just hearing the boy consider cutting his hair had me feeling pretty good. That hair of his was bone of contention with me from the beginning.

"I'm down, dude. Let's do this."

"Cool!"

We slapped hands. I watched him settle back into his lounging position, but he wasn't through with me yet. He studied me hard like something else was on his mind.

"So," he asked, "how you and Uncle Smoke hook up?"

Smoke jumped in. "We boys from way back. Willie here lived down the street from me, although we wouldn't start kicking it till well after high school. I was the cat everybody wanted to be, you know--"Mack Daddy big pimping", like y'all say. Pretty much doing the same things you young'uns think you got ownership rights to. Me and Willie B, we the 'Original Gangsters'."

"Yeah, that's true. Your uncle here always had the gift of gab, which just means he could talk shit with the best and back it up. I was a scrawny young thing, quiet but tough. Smoke was always trying to get my dandruff up," I laughed, "but I wasn't buying."

"My boy Gene and I are like that," Tyrell said digging into earth with a small stick, "and Ron--the dude who died--we was all tight. Man, I miss my homies, but it's gonna be good to see Gene again...hang out with him.

Grandma says he been looking for me. I'm gonna check him out when we get back."

I watched this boy, as if I was watching a film of myself being played backward, given the chance to begin again. I wanted to hold him, to mold him, to let him know it was okay to fuck up once and again...More importantly, even when you fucked up, there was someone there to pick you up. I saw so much of myself in him that, at times. I didn't know where he began and I ended.

In just two days, I would be driving young Tyrell to Charlotte, North Carolina. Smoke had another sister who lived there, married with two kids. She was a little reluctant at first, but agreed to allow Tyrell to live with her family. Tyrell didn't have a clue about the trip or his permanent change of residence.

"You a good kid," Bebe said, "You family. You" Bebe pointed to each one of us, then clasped her chest, "my family."

No truer words had been spoken and to hear it coming out of Bebe's mouth, I liken to an angel's harp--the purest expression of love.
Tyrell leaned over and kissed her on the cheek. Smoke patted his back, and gave me a wink and some dap.

We sat there in them woods a little while longer. It seems like no one wanted to ever leave.

***

The day of reckoning was upon us. Smoke concocted some elaborate lie and had the good fortune of the boy believing him. Tyrell was reluctant at first, but in the few weeks he had come to know us, he also had come to trust us. We gave him a few hours to spend with his grandma and gather some of his personal things, and then I was to pick him up and drive him to North Carolina. Smoke couldn't make the ride because of his leg--at least that's what he told us--but I knew that he just didn't want to face saying goodbye...and, quiet as it's kept, neither did I.

"Alright, Willie man, y'all have a safe trip and call me once you reach Charlotte. Then I can give Sheila a call and let her know you will be on your way. You know how she is--she don't like no surprises, and although--we go way back, she swear she don't remember you."

"It's all good, Smoke. I got this. We are gonna do fine."

Smoke shook his head then looked around his bar. "Man, I don't know. I'm thinking about making a move myself. This place ain't like it used to be. It's missing," he paused..."something."

"You will shutdown Smokes Bar and Grill? No way! The fella's ain't having it. Man, this is history."

"Yeah, I know, Willie, but I'm tired...and this thing with Juan G--well, it just had me thinking--this week, it's him...next week, it's some other fool. I have done enough partying here to last a life time. But, I can't deny; it sure was some good times."

"The best!"

My eyes followed his as I reminisced about the time spent at Smoke's place, hanging with the crux of the Civil Rights movement, the elite and the underground elite, all in one place, one common goal--to have a good time. Sure, we had our beefs, but, in the end, we worked them out. We stood for the community; we stood for each other. I guess that's what was missing.

"Look, you better get going. You all need to be on the road before sunset. It's a long drive."

"Alright, Smoke, I'll call you when we get there."

We hugged...like brothers.

***

I dropped Tyrell off at his grandma's. I gave him a few hours to tie up a few last strings and say goodbye. Me--I didn't really have no where to go, so I circled the block for a few then grabbed some lunch. To tell you the truth, I was ready to get on the road and be done with this whole thing. It wouldn't work out that way.

I pulled back in front of Tyrell's grandma's house. Everything was as it appeared when I left--screen door open, fan blowing--but when I knocked, no one answered. I took it upon myself to enter the house. I wasn't a threat or anything, but I took precautions, hollering out Tyrell's name and his grandma's as I made my way through the house. My knocks, my yells went unanswered until I found Tyrell's grandma hollering, screaming and carrying on.

"Where's Tyrell?" I asked.

"He gone. My baby's *gone*."

"Where?"

"Gone to find his daddy!"

"His daddy? Smoke?"

"Yeah, he gone to find Smoke. I didn't tell him; he heard it from someone on the street, and now he all mad about it. He wouldn't listen to me. He don't listen to no one."

I knew if Tyrell knew or found out that Smoke was his real father, then it would only complicate things. We were supposed to be on the road far, far away from here and harm, but now things had changed for the worse. If Juan G found out that Tyrell was still in town, it could be the death of all of us.

***

I drove through lights and intersections. Rushing. Anticipating the worst.

Visions of shots fired.

Smoke on the ground.

Blood...so much blood.

Beep! Beep! A horn blared.

Tyrell.

Smoke.

I couldn't think--just react. I reached under the seat; my gat was still there, fully loaded.

I made the turn into Smoke's place. Shut off the engine, then rushed up to the door, my gat ready, slammed against sweaty palms and trigger-happy fingers.

"Smoke, you okay?"

"Yeah man, what's up with you? Tyrell!" he hollered. "Uncle Willie's here--you ready to go?"

Everything was okay--but not okay. My eyes searched the room like spotlights, looking for anything out of place, out of sync.

"You alright?" I asked.

"Damn, Willie, what's got you spooked? I was just saying goodbye to Tyrell."

"Tyrell!" I hollered. "Come on, man, we got to go!"

"I'm coming!" he hollered from the back.

But, for the life of me, I couldn't figure out why he was out back. Why was he in Smoke's office? The hairs on my neck were standing still and upright; something wasn't right.

"Tyrell! Get moving, we got to book!"

Smoke looked at me like I was crazed or something.

"What's up, Willie?"

I looked around, expecting something to jump off at any time.

"It's cool Smoke. Just want to get the boy to somewhere safe."

Smoke turned toward the bar and back room and hollered again.

"Tyrell! Come on dude! You got your uncle waiting."

Silence.

I didn't hear the first bullet, or maybe I didn't recognize it for what it was. It whizzed past me, striking Smoke in the shoulder, and he fell to the ground.

Tyrell ran and dived behind Smoke in the midst of gunfire. I pulled my gat and fired, not knowing who or what I was shooting at. Bebe howled from her stool, screaming at the top her lungs. I wanted to save her, but I couldn't because I couldn't see who or what I was shooting at.

"It's over, Smoke. O-V-E-R, over. I told you to get that little nigga out! Naw, y'all want to mess around and bullshit me! Now you got to pay the price. Now, everyone dies."

Juan G pulled another gun from his hip and began shooting. I didn't know where Smoke or Tyrell was. I fired from behind the bar, hoping I took him out.

Five minutes later the entire room was filled with gun smoke. I waited, crouched behind the bar, for the next bullet and sounds of the living but I heard nothing...only silence. Then Bebe began to sing.

I crawled out from behind the bar to access the damage. Nobody moved. My heart hung in my hands as I made my way to Smoke lying prone on the floor.

"Damn! Smoke!" I shook and tried to turn him over. His eyes were fixated on nothing; his mouth was bleeding; and his body was one big bullet wound. My heart wrenched.

"Smoke?"

I knew, even as I spoke his name he was gone.

There was so much blood, I couldn't see where the wound began or ended, just a big red target on Smoke's chest. "Aw shit, Smoke!" I hugged my friend and held him near me--wishing for him to breathe, to laugh one more time--but I heard nothing but my own whimpering.

"I'm sorry Unc. It's all my fault."

My eyes finally found and rested on Tyrell sitting in the far corner near the juke box. I was happy to see him, more than happy, until I saw the gun between his hands.

"What you do, boy? What you do?!" I cried.

The boy shook his head. "He was my daddy. Smoke was my daddy; that's what Ma told me. Why couldn't y'all just tell me that? Why y'all have to keep it hidden from me?"

I lifted myself off the ground and stood in front of Tyrell, but he wouldn't look at me. He just looked down at his shoes splattered with blood and cried.

"I didn't want to shoot him...but he was gonna kill me."

My heart ached for the familiar; the smell of smoked ribs, the sounds of an old juke box; Smokes loud voice and his hearty laughter. The memories faded like sands in an hourglass. All that remained was us, the family--Smokes family and yet, I still felt empty.

Bebe sat so still on her stool that I thought she was dead, too, but she let out a shrill so piercing, it shook the world beneath us.

"My fam-i-ly!" she screamed. "My fam-i-ly!"

Juan G lay at the door in a pool of blood, no doubt his own.

I heard the sirens and knew I had to act fast; all of our lives depended on it.

"Tyrell, give me the gun."

He hesitated.

"Give me the gun!"

Tyrell didn't move.

"Now, Tyrell!"

This time he heard me, and let the piece drop from his hands into mine.

I wiped the gun clean and placed it in Smoke's hand. It would be what he wanted. This, I knew for sure

"Tyrell, get Bebe. We got to go!"

***

It was a perfect spring day in June that I decided to make my second trip to North Carolina. With Bebe by my side, we drove the six hours straight--only one stop, for gas. Our conversation was limited since Bebe didn't talk much, but she sang all the way. Her voice is what I needed.

We pulled up into the parking lot. I helped Bebe out and showed her to a seat next to me. She sat silently rocking back and forth, while my leg trembled underneath me. I tried to rationalize this feeling of anxiety, this feeling of maybe being in the wrong place for all the right reasons, but no answers came that would satisfy me or make me relinquish my seat. I was here because I was meant to be here. We were family.

When Smoke was laid to rest I made a promise to myself, Bebe and Tyrell that I would look after them forevermore and I did. I moved Bebe in with me and cared for her like my own sister. I wrote to Tyrell and kept in touch with his aunt to make sure he was doing the right thing, and all was good. I can proudly say I lived up to my promise, and now--today--Tyrell fulfilled a promise to us.

"Tyrell Davis," the announcer called.

I gleamed with joy and Bebe hollered as Tyrell took the stage, accepting his diploma, dancing a jig, and shouting to his friends and family. It was the day we all waited for. It is what Smoke and I hoped for since the day we laid eyes on him. We wanted to save him.

***

"What up, Uncle?" Tyrell reached for me, hugging me tightly.

"You my boy!" I hugged him back. "Your daddy would have been proud."

It was kind of an awkward moment for us all as we stood in silence, remembering Smoke--me wishing he was here.

"He loved you son."

"I know. Without you and Smoke, I wouldn't be here."

Sheila, Smoke's sister hollered, "Turn around! Let me get a picture."

So, the three of us wrapped arms around each other and posed.

"My fam-i-ly", Bebe said smiling, "My fam-i-ly."

Love

I have loved
I have loved beyond color
Beyond lines
I have loved
I have loved when I was tired
And lacking
And wanting more
I have loved.
I have loved when he did not,
When he needed more time
When he didn't know what he wanted
I have loved up and down and through and above
The intricacies of love
I know
Cause I have wanted love, hated love, needed love
Known love, spoke with and of love
And still, I have not had enough
I have loved.

Brandy L. McCrary

Toss – A – Cross
By Torrance Stephens

There is nothing more certain than that a man will be a man, and that for his seed, he is the first line of defense...if there is no dog outside. The simple truth is that such a person is never off guard; his only fear is not being able to feed and provide for his children. Unfortunately, this makes such an individual diabolical and sinister--the worse attributes for anyone who feels that all his children have in the world to protect them is his strength.

It was one of those nights in between spring and summer, but this night seemed more reflective of winter than either of the aforementioned. The only difference was that, unlike winter months, the sun could still be seen allocating pastel hues into the cloudless and anticipating dark. The crickets were also in full sonic bloom; as if they were some species of perennial audibly calling nature to order, and it was time now for the rest of the flowers to catch up. The flowering trees stood at attention, good soldiers in an eternal precision drill of beautiful growth, obeying the crickets' chirped command. They always seemed to be the first to bloom, after the bulbs, and they flowered in the order of the pink and purple crab apple tree, the white of the pear trees and the opaque shades of the box woods--which were really shrubs, but in his yard, the bushes were the height of a tree.

He was outside as usual. It was beverage time and a good time to just enjoy life for its own sake. His cup held no distillate of the Agave plant but rather, this time, sake-- sake and a 24 ounce can of Tecate beer. He walked out onto the "chat-rock" gravel road. In any urban area outside his Georgia residence, it would be a driveway, with the exception that it was 110 yards from his house. He, Jones, Mac Jones often marveled at the oddity of the distance, since it seemed strange...even to a Memphis nigga.

Mac walked inside; his glass was empty. His son and daughter were in his son's room. The boy was making music while his sister was bellowing into the microphone. Unintelligible certainly, nonetheless she was jamming. Mac peeked in then decided he'd walk to his room on the other side of the dwelling. The house was large and gave any stranger the semblance that the 4,000 square feet was divided into wings. Upon seeing daddy, Mac's daughter followed quickly, as quickly as any child a few months before the age of two could waddle in a straight line. To Mac, she walked like Bobby Cox.

On his floor in front of the muted television, Mac Jones sat down and began folding clothes. He had been at work since early morning, and his son's baseball game was rained out. Thank goodness for leftovers. But before he could finish the towels, his princess Bobby Coxed in. She only had a few words in her vocabulary, but affection was what she communicated best. Crawling over him and placing her head on his chest, she wrapped her legs around his and started to go to sleep.

When she went to sleep, Mac got up from the floor and placed his precious girl down for the night. Again he returned outside, to the crickets and the night air. The stars seemed to talk to him, but he could not decide if it was the stars or the sake.

He looked over by his fruit tree. The backhoe was still there. The plumber needed it to replace the drainage pipe--$1700.00 worth of pipe. The thought of the cost made him sick at the stomach. But, he had the lot, and it made his property better, more valuable he was told, if he replaced the pipe. Mac worked hard for his dollar--no slavery, just hard work--and he could handle the cost if it improved his castle...especially for his children's sake. The queen mother--well, she earned her exile from home and its comforts. He had just broken up with his woman. All he could repeat to himself was their last verbal exchange.

"I'm gone have someone come out her and take care of you," she said, somewhere in between a manic rage and cynical rant." Well send them on," *Mac said, coolly while raising the nature of the threat. "If they come out here, let them play cowboy...and I'll make it the Okay* **Corral***."*

He erased that from his mind and looked again to the stars. The night's emissaries of peace made him feel full, removing the restive anxiety, while leaving Mac placated and at ease--a feeling he had not felt in a while. He walked down the gravel driveway, sipping a fresh cup of sake. A few rabbits ran-hopped across his path, but Mac was undisturbed by their presence. He sat patiently in his stance looking at the pine trees around him and the cars passing by.

It was strange to him, at this time of night, to see the lights of a vehicle turn in his direction. Maybe it happened all the time; perhaps he was just outside at the right time. This vehicle did not seem like the others, as if it was a mistake--an accident. But, maybe it was, for they waited and dimmed the lights. *Maybe they're being respectful,* he thought. Nonetheless, he went to his truck and pulled his yellow bag from under the passenger seat and returned to his musing spot. He had anticipated that the vehicle would have backed up and turned around by now, but it had not. They, that vehicle's occupants, were still there, silently sitting, speaking an unspoken threat. So, he stood, shoulders square and head high, as if to provide the nonverbal locution that this was his property-- Mac Jones' property.

The men in the late model Chevy approached slowly and then sped up briefly before stopping. One man got out. "Hey...who live here...you live here?"

Mac said nothing; just looked, without visible emotion.

"Yo Nigga, I'm talking to you...this your place?"

"*Main*, you in no position to ask, not to mention...you must be a fool."

"A fool...who you calling a *fool?*"

Mac pointed to the sign right below one of the many cameras on his land. It read 'TRESPASSERS WILL BE SHOT'.

"Nigga, I can read, and I ain't scared." He raised his shirt, revealing the .380 pistol that was tucked in his pants. Mac laughed.

"What you laughing at? You don't know who you fucking with, nigga."

"Naw... I don't, but not only are you a fool, but you are obviously a bitch too...totin' around that bitch pistol." Mac laughed but continued, "Why you on my property...who you looking for...hell, while you hea', would you like some sake?

"I'm looking for you."

"*Jones... main*, you don't know me to look for me."

You 'Mac Jones', ain't you? Your old lady asked us to pay you a visit."

"OK...and?"

"You don't recognize me. I'm a rapper, *main*--I've been in videos and shit."

"Nope, can't say I have, *jones.*"

"You heard of 'Welcome to Murda Valley,' *main?*" Mac shook his head in the negative. "That's my song, *shawty.*"

Then, it clicked: *My old lady sent him.* He knew that she was incapable of reason, but such should have been expected from a distorted and psychotic mind. Mac backed up slowly. The young *jones* continued to approach Mac; this *jones* was short and fronted as if he was hard as concrete, and he was black, so black Mac could barely see him if not for the shine of the parking lights from his vehicle and the glimmer of the moon off "Mr. Murda Valley's" yellow teeth.

The short, black *jones* opened the door to the car and said something to the other two men that accompanied him. Closing the door, he approached Mac. It was a slow approach, one that showed he was uncertain of himself and of what he was about to get into. He looked backed toward the car and laughed, then more assertively approached, like he was the one who owned the land, or as if the bravado gained during the drive over had made his testicles fortified with steel.

"Is you or ain't you Mac Jones, nigga?"

"Yep," Mac said, finishing his sake. "Well, I came to tell you something."

"You can stand where you are and talk, sir."

"Naw... can't do that, *folk.*"

"I ain't yo' *'folk'*!" Mac said, sternly. "*Main*, you pathetic! You come on my property, insult me— no— first trespass, come without invite, turn down my offer to beverage...not to mention, my children are inside asleep, and you expect me to talk to you. Can't do it, *main*, but I *can* make you my ho and, afterwards, send **your** black ass to pre-K--'cause it is obvious to me you a dumb ass fuck boy. You come up in *my* camp 'cause some woman thinks *you* hard, and *you* think you hard. You fake ass wanna-be gangster," Mac laughed hardy and insultingly.

"Whoop that nigga's ass," came roughly from the car.

The "fuck boy" continued his walk. As he approached, he began to pull something from his shirt, a menacing move meant to send a message without true violent action—but terribly foolhardy. Mac sized up the young maverick. Suddenly, the young thug surged toward Mac and took a wild swing at him. As he swung, Mac sidestepped, dropping his little yellow bag, popped a hard right fist into *folk's* jaw, and then followed with a "down South hay-maker" from his left hand that crushed into the opposite jaw. Mac was taught by his uncle that the best punch was neither the straight punch to the face nor an upper cut to the chin, but rather a fully-balled fist swung like a club to an opponent's face. It had the stopping power of a truck. Mac taught "Mr. Murder Valley" this same lesson.

As the "young buck" stumbled, Mac grabbed him behind his neck and kneed him in his chin, then immediately grabbed his head and snapped his neck like a dry twig. "Short and black" dropped dead to the gravel driveway's dusty, rough surface.

The remaining opponents, angered by their partner's violent end, jumped out the Chevy pulling weapons from under their shirts. Mac chuckled at the "movie stunt"--he would never tuck a "gat" in his pants, aiming it at his dick and scrotum--and deftly reached for the yellow bag. Mac rolled quickly behind a magnolia tree before the would-be shooters could aim, bag in hand. Picking up a seedpod from the same tree, he pulled out the

.44 magnum from the bag, slammed the pod on his barrel and fired two shots. Two heavy thuds--both men dropped.

Mac rolled over, farther away from the action, breathing deeply and holding his chest. He never knew he was that proficient with a handgun. In fact, he preferred rifles and was taught growing up that if he needed a pistol, he was probably too close. He was impressed with himself, even surprised, but the gun was a Magnum, and the slug was expected to go through a little plastic subcompact car and the glass.

Mac looked at the three corpses on his gravel road. *This wasn't no killin'...this was protectin' what was mine,* Mac reasoned within as he checked his Magnum, putting on the safety. It was completely dark now; once again, he could hear the crickets. He dragged "rapper dude" to the opposite side of the pear trees, and then returned to the vehicle and stuffed the other two bodies back into the auto. Mac, showing no mercy, drove the car over the first body and parked.

Walking as if he had no care in the world, he went to the house to check on his children. They were sound asleep. Mac returned outside and went to the backhoe. Starting the backhoe's engine, he began to dig a new hole. It took him almost two hours, but he had managed to build a hole big enough to bury the auto seven feet below the surface. He had hardly worked up a sweat thanks to modern technology, hydraulics, and the spirited night breeze. He moved the backhoe in position behind the auto and carefully climbed off the construction machine. Next, he placed the remaining corpse in the car and positioned the car right in front of the hole. Placing the car in neutral, he used the backhoe to push it in the hole.

It was easier to cover the vehicle, compared to digging the hole. Stopping, Mac grabbed his yellow bag and, using the material of the pouch, wiped then threw the gun into the auto's open window. He figured that by leaving the windows open, the bodies would decompose faster and larva would have an easier time to get to them. As for the gun, it was a throwaway, a "toss-across", as they used to say back in Memphis. It was only meant for one-time use.

He and his boys always joked that he had enough land to bury somebody and their car. Now he chuckled briefly at the irony. A Libertarian, Mac knew he was not the kind of guy who would call 911. He did not need the government to protect him.

Satisfied that he was finished, he pulled a Kool Mild cigarette from his pants pocket and lit it. He repositioned the back hoe and climbed down from its perch. Again, he looked toward the sky. Now, all that was left to do was take a shower, get some rest and prepare his children for school in the morning. On the way home from work, he would purchase a few boxes of daffodil bulbs, maybe a few lilies, and some lavender to take root in his new flower bed.

AmaSong

I was given burst by the Creator

Nursed and fed on my mother

Was taught the initials of l-i-f-e at play with my father

Acknowledged the word *love* for the sake of my brothers

Forgave and accepted alongside my sisters

The world schooled me in terms of dread and protection--among
others

And in spite on myself

I became

Part protector/ part dread

Part sister/ part brother

Part father/ part mother

Part creator--among others

Part trickster/ fool/ charmer

Part...Man

I am a man

A man borne for you

A man in deed for the cause of you

I am a man because the cause of you has become the cause of me

For that --and more-- I want you now

For that --and more-- I wed you then

I wed you Orisha eyes and African spirit

Your soul-filled politics and flowering compassion

I marry you ever-unfolding beauty and relaxed un-pretention

I marry you with love through misunderstanding and discomfort

Ill-spoken words, unredeemable deeds

And when the rains come

I will find shelter for you and not from you

And when the sun shines

I will bask in the glow with you and not in spite of you

I marry you for something borrowed and blue

Something older than this moment

Something newer than tomorrow

I marry for something as ephemeral as a flame

Something always stretching always and never

Something whether or not

I marry you for what we have

And all the what we ain't got

I marry you for something not unlike the love I feel today

Something not unlike the love I will feel from today

Always and Forever

This I swear

Orande Ash

Dedication

I want to dedicate this project to my wife, Michelle, and my kids, Tameika, Brittanie, Melanie, Michaila and Miles. Everything I endeavor to do, I do to make your lives better. You all mean the world to me.

Deborah.
Thanks for the
Love and support.

R. Fitz

One to Remember
By R. Fitzgerald

Giving of one's heart is never an easy thing to do, especially for a man. In fact, most men would rather opt for a life of sex than to truly give their heart over to a woman and have it broken into pieces. But, sometimes, love is spontaneous, and the heart doesn't forewarn you of its intentions; it simply succumbs. Everett knew this all too well. The moment he saw Samaya James, his heart stopped. She was the one. Everything within him confirmed it. Yet, here it was, nearly thirty-six hours since Samaya left Atlanta for her return trip home, and he couldn't fathom why she hadn't called. All sorts of questions began racing through Everett's mind.

Does she feel the same way I do about her? Maybe she hasn't called because she is studying for her finals? Or, maybe she's there with "them," laughing at me. Maybe, this was all some big joke. A way to get back at me for all the dirt I've done in the past. Nah, that couldn't be it. She's not that type of girl. She would never do something like that.

His mind kept vacillating until he made a conscious effort to reassure himself that all was well. Besides, his playing days were behind him. He had to be out of karma's reach by now, or, at least he hoped so. Their time together had been genuine; Everett refused to believe anything less.

Regardless of whether it was coincidental or intentional, Ms. James hadn't called, and it was beginning to bother him. Everett wrestled within himself on whether he should leave yet another message; he was already up to three. He wanted to be cool but also caring. If she wasn't feeling the same way about him -- there he was, doubting himself again -- he wanted to restrain his emotions. The problem: he already played his hand. It was too late to renege. He could feel love rising inside of him, and it was about to spill over. Anticipating the return of her love had him open. All she had to do was say the word, and he was hers -- forever.

Samaya managed to accomplish in a matter of weeks what some had worked months to achieve, but to no avail. Maybe it was timing, or, maybe it was the newness of love; but, whatever it was, Everett was sick over her. Literally. His body was filled with angst. He was sure the warm radiance of love didn't feel like this. This sensation was more akin to a sickening, creeping feeling; an evasive nervousness that caused his heart to engage in rhythmic abandon. Panic, no doubt. He could feel it closing in like a speeding car in a rearview mirror, and, as the hours since her departure continued to escalate, he became a ball of nerves. He needed to hear her voice. He needed to know she was free from harm. He needed her to dishevel the thoughts that consumed him. He needed to know...that she, too...was falling in love.

Chapter 2

The eve of conception – summer of 93'

"Yo, Everett! Yo, Derrick!" Rob yelled from the asphalt parking lot. He was trotting in the direction of his "boyz," Everett Goins and Derrick Roberts. The two friends had wandered onto the turf-covered field just off the Norman Hall parking lot. They were on the campus of University of Florida, Everett's alma mater, catching up on old times now that the frat party held in Norman Gym was letting out. Everett and Derrick turned to see Rob Jenkins jogging in their direction while throwing up his hand, motioning to them to wait up.

"What's up fellas?" Rob said as he extended his hand to Everett for a "pound": their fists connected top and bottom in a duplicitous motion followed by the tapping of knuckles to the middle. Rob repeated the same greeting with Derrick as they exchanged the brotherly greetings of "whatup dawg" and "good to see you". The guys had known each other since Everett's sophomore year, when they all lived in Broward Hall.

"So, what's going on man?" Rob said.

"Nothing much...just catching up with Derrick. What's been up with you?"

"Same ole, same ole: just working, kicking it, and trying to get up on a few of these ladies in the process. So, what brings you to town?"

"I'm just here taking care of a little Army Reserve business, but, now that I have that out the way, I figured I'd take a stroll on campus."

"Well, you should have come a little earlier because you missed a good party. The honeys were out in mass tonight."

"Yeah, well, I just wanted to see a few faces. I'm not into partying as much as I used to be," Everett responded.

"That's hard to believe. I figured with you being in Atlanta, you'd be kicking it nonstop. I guess a couple years out of school make a big difference," Derrick added.

"Well, if you remember correctly, I started making my descent before I left Gainesville. I still get out, but now, it's in the form of concerts, festivals and plays. You know…adult fun."

"I can dig that, but we don't get much of that here…so I guess we'll have to settle for chasing hoes," Derrick said engaging them in a hearty laugh.

"So, check it: What are the ladies like in Atlanta? I hear it's eleven to one. Those are some nice odds," Rob said.

"It's probably higher than that, but for real, you couldn't tell; it's still hard to find a good woman. There are a lot of fine chicks in Atlanta, but a lot of them are looking for a sponsor; and I'm not looking to take on baggage. I work too hard for my money."

"I hear you on that, but does that mean you ain't tapping nothing?" Rob inquired.

"Come on now. This is *Everett* you're talking to. I can run 'em with the best of 'em, but I'm tired of macking. I'm looking to settle down."

"I feel you on that," Derrick responded "I'd like to find my better half as well, but that's easier said than done."

"Man, we're still young. Ya'll better do like me and get all you can, while you can," Rob said.

"Been there; done that, dawg. I've had enough for you, me and the next man. Sooner or later, we all have to grow up. It's more to life than just chasing."

***

Circa 1991

The spoils of the game were not as fulfilling as Everett had hoped. Not only was there a horrible taste in his mouth, but he was obese with disappointment. Playing the game to win had backfired. His life had somehow transformed into a cautionary tale, and he had morphed into a lower form of man. He had become his own worst enemy; he was a "ho." At least, that's what *they* called him. Sure, he had done the deeds. Since he kept his mouth closed and made his moves at night, he thought that his unseemly conduct would remain in the dark. He never considered that his demise would be the result of his bedmates' inability to keep their mouths closed. To think, all he wanted was a girl to call his own.

Now that the shoe was on the other foot, Everett hated the word "ho." At least being called a "playa" had a nice ring to it. But a ho? That just didn't sit well with him. That inferred that he didn't have any qualifications for the women he slept with, that he hit everything that came his way, which was farther from the truth: he only went after the cute girls. Well...maybe a few nice-bodied ugly ones, but no one knew about those -- or so he thought.

Anyway, he learned early on that most of the guys avoided the really attractive ladies because they assumed they were unattainable. That made them the least sought after girls on campus -- highly desired, but the least sought after. Most of the guys were running after the middle-of-the-road girls, the fairly attractive girls with nice bodies.

A guy would easily choose a girl with B-grade attractiveness, as long as she had an A-grade personality, and, sometimes, that was negotiable. Domestic skills were also a plus, and - for most- ATTITUDE would not be tolerated.

Everett didn't want to settle; he wanted top shelf, definitely A-grade attractiveness. Unlike some guys, he wouldn't just accept a girl based on physical attributes alone. He knew that a fine woman represented the pinnacle amongst men -- and having one by your side spoke volumes -- but he wanted more than just the superficial. After dating quite a few women, he found that a lot of the pretty girls were just that -- surface pretty, a face to be put on display. No domestic skills to speak of, boring, no form of intelligent conversation, few interests other than themselves, and, at times, expensive. Subsequently, Everett went through a lot of women; secretly he was looking for his soul mate. And, as strange as it may sound for a "playa," he wanted a woman that would cause him to thank God for her on a daily basis, a woman who could be the mother of his children, the love of his life; a woman he could love to the limits of his heart -- and then some -- if she could endure it.

The funny thing about desire is that it is usually just a goal we have in mind. Everett's desire was no different because, somewhere along the way, he ended up settling for sex while looking for love. He engaged in so much sex that he lost his ability to discern love. He couldn't decide which end was up. So, it was hard for him to trust the emotions of the girl who fell in love quickly, even if he liked her. He wanted to feel special but couldn't help thinking she was probably this way with other guys. He didn't want some girl who was just as dysfunctional emotionally as he was. How could he trust that? If he settled for a girl like that, what would become of it?

Enough ground had already been lost. He needed to regroup. It was time to disappear from the social scene and just concentrate on graduating. Maybe, time would make things right. Maybe, love would find him. He knew something had to give because, for all his trying, taking matters into his own hands was undoubtedly failing him.

***

The eve, revisited

The walk back to his car was a short distance - no longer than a football field, but it was taking Everett quite a bit of time to get to his destination. He had a five-hour drive ahead of him the following day, and he was ready to retire for the evening. However, as he made the trek across the blacktop, he continually encountered names and faces he recognized from him days as a student. His southern upbringing would not allow him just to walk by without at least a hello, so he felt obligated to engage a few people. The conversations were all the same.
"What's up?"
"Nothing much"
"How've you been?"
"Fine."
"What are you doing now?"
Blah, Blah, Blah. His mind was more on leaving than on the faces that found themselves in front of him. That is, until his stride was broken by the voice of Samaya James.
"Hi, Everett," she said, as she stepped away from the group of Delta sisters with whom she was "hanging".

"Samaya?" he said, not believing his eyes. He greeted her with a hug; the standard greeting amongst the sexes on campus. He hadn't seen her in years but he was immediately re-attracted to her, just like the first time he saw her. She looked better now. Her body, a poetic sight: chocolate butter skin, lavish legs, arms like Angela -- Bassett, of course -- bountiful breasts, and her butt -- not too big, but capable of getting the job done. Her hair was different as well. Gone was the jheri curl. Instead, she wore a feathered cut; cropped in the back - excellent choice of style. Add the loss of about ten pounds, and he found it hard for his eyes not to linger. *She was beautiful,* he thought. *Someone I could never forget.*

The only reason he hadn't stepped to her in the past was his friend, Kenyan Cooper. Kenyan introduced Everett and Samaya during her sophomore year, two years prior. Kenyan was a fellow "playa" who also had a girlfriend at the time, but Everett knew Kenyan was keeping Samaya on ice...just in case. It was something in the way he introduced her. "She's a good girl...the kind of girl you want to marry," Everett remembered Kenyan saying. As he stood admiring her, he wondered if Kenyan still kept in touch with her. Everett had not seen or talked to him since they graduated; he had not really thought about him much till now. The more his eyes traveled the length of her body, the more he concluded that she was looking too good to pass up. Kenyan had graduated and moved on, but here she was, looking lovely as ever -- which is exactly why he ignored the thought to stand down.

"What a pleasant surprise. If my memory serves me well, you didn't do a lot of parties. So, what brings you out tonight?" Everett responded.

"Oh, I'm just hanging with my sorors. I still don't hang out much, but I only have two classes this summer;

so that allows me to take a break every now and then. So, what brings you to town?"

"I'm just here handling some paperwork so that I can switch Army Reserve units. I'm tired of making the five-hour drive once a month, so I figured it was high time I made the switch to a unit in Atlanta. But, enough about me, I see you pledged Delta since I left. Congratulations. What else have I missed?"

"Nothing spectacular -- just studying, for the most part. I'm actually taking classes this summer so that I can graduate next May. I'm so ready to put this part of my life behind me."

"I know what you mean. I couldn't wait to graduate, and now that I have, life is pretty good. I surely don't miss all the studying, and its good not having to depend on my parents for money."

As the two carried on in conversation, Everett got the feeling that this was the opportunity he had been waiting for. Not only was Samaya smart -- an engineering major -- but her conversation was engaging, energetic and full of passion. She was a breath of fresh air, and he was becoming lost in their time together, lost in the movement of her lips -- lips he hoped to kiss in the not too distant future. The more he thought about it, the less of her conversation he comprehended. Her voice was slowly becoming background noise, but he instinctively kept smiling and nodding until he regained his awareness. When he did, he realized he owed it to himself to seize this moment.

"So, I just have to ask, are you seeing anybody? I'd love to call you sometime."

Everett knew women loved confident guys, guys with a little swagger about themselves and just enough bravado so they didn't come across cocky.

"No. Nobody ever tries to talk to me. The only thing I get to see is my books. I actually was starting to wonder if something was wrong with me."

"Oh, definitely not! If there is a problem, then it must be the guys here because from where I'm standing, things look mighty nice."

Samaya blushed. Everett was off to a good start. He was glad no one was in the picture. That made it easier for him.

Go ahead. Act like you're the man, he told himself.

Everett reached in his blazer pocket for a pen then patted down his jeans until he found a piece of paper in his pocket. "If you give me your number, I'll be sure and call you when I get back to Atlanta, and I promise not to play the "three-day waiting" game with you," he said, smiling.

"Well...only if you give me yours also," she said.

"By all means," he said. *You can have anything you like,* he thought. She looked up from writing her number. He could tell she liked him coming on to her. Her smile lit up the night as she handed him the pen and paper. While they exchanged gazes and smiles, his mind reverted back to Kenyan. *Damn,* he thought, *Why do I have to be thinking about that brother?* He felt as if he were stepping on Kenyan's toes. Kenyan and he were "cool as fans," and Kenyan was one of the few guys Everett admired and respected during his school days. Had it been anyone else, Everett probably would not have given talking to Samaya a second thought. He wanted to ignore the feeling, but Kenyan was a stand-up dude. If Everett was going to engage in a relationship with Samaya, then he wanted it to be cool with Kenyan. As much as he liked his chances, Everett had to pay respect to the game. This situation fell under one of those unwritten rules amongst men: Never step to one of your partner's women -- unless he was just hitting it -- and then, you still needed his permission.

So, when was the last time you talked to Kenyan?" he finally asked.

"It's been a while, but we keep in touch from time to time," she said.

"You two ever date?" he asked. For the first time during their conversation, he felt the energy change. *That's not a good sign*, he thought.

"We thought about it, but he admitted that he wasn't ready for anything serious so we've just maintained a friendship." It wasn't the definitive answer Everett was looking for; it was a bit too open ended for his taste. He didn't want to come across as presumptuous, but he had to say it.

"You know, we are "boyz." I can't really cross any lines with you, if it's not cool with him."

She looked at him. He searched her expression to see if she was offended but realized that she seemed to understand. "I don't think that will be a problem."

"I hope not," he said earnestly, "I'd really like to get to know you better."

For now he'd accept her response, but he knew he'd have to revisit this matter of Kenyan later...especially if things really started to take off.

"Samaya, we're *ready*," sang a voice, one that Everett immediately recognized. When he looked in the direction of the voice, there stood Nashi Simpson. *She's still fine*, Everett thought. And, from the looks of it she was one of Samaya's sorority sisters. He was so caught up in how fine Samaya was looking, he hadn't noticed any of the other Delta's standing nearby.

"Hi, Everett, how are you doing?" she asked.

"I'm fine," he said while nodding his head in acknowledgement to her greeting.

He hadn't expected to see her tonight. She was an old crush that never took flight and seeing Nashi and Samaya in the same circle was making him a bit uneasy. Everett eyed the approaching group of ladies behind Nashi and noticed other winsome faces. The Delta's at UF had made a "come-up" during Everett's time on campus! It was no longer the organization only for the "Sista Big Bones" on campus. No sir! All the fine mademoiselles, whether thick, petite, light or dark, who didn't consider themselves bourgeois enough to be AKA's were pledging Delta. So, when Tiffany stepped through the crowd of ladies, his stomach plummeted. *She's a Delta too! This might not be so good after all*, he thought.

Tiffany and Everett had been "friends with benefits" a few years back. Mind you, they were not a public item; they just had a deep sexual attraction that they indulged on more than one occasion. Everett abruptly ended their exchange due to some rather strange extenuating circumstances: he found it necessary to confess to Tiffany that he wanted to approach a young lady he had a crush on. His intentions were to make this new woman his lady. Not that Tiffany wasn't worthy of the same, but the truth of the matter was that she wasn't looking for a man -- she already had one. Everett needed her to know they couldn't be "friends" any longer because the person he was interested in was someone Tiffany knew very well. In fact, it was Tiffany's next-door neighbor and current sorority sister, Nashi. Tiffany had to admit that she admired his respect for her feelings. So, she gave him her blessing and went a step further by informing Nashi of his interests -- a token of appreciation for some *jobs well done*, no doubt.

What Everett did not factor into the equation was Nashi's response. She was totally uncomfortable with the whole idea. He sensed her tension the first day that he came to visit her. She thought he was a nice enough guy, but she knew of his clandestine visits with Tiffany; and this arrangement was just too close for comfort. She didn't get down like that. In hindsight, Everett realized it was a noble approach but not one of his smarter moves.

Knowing those three ladies would be together tonight increased Everett's apprehensiveness. He felt his past might very well be coming back to haunt him. His chances were still looking pretty good, but he didn't want to push it. So, he decided lingering was no longer in his best interest.

"Hey, don't let me hold you. I'll call you when I get back home. I'm glad I ran into you."

He scribbled down his number, ripped it off the paper, and handed it to her. He did, however, take the time to give her a hug goodnight.

"It was really nice seeing you; I'll talk with you later," she said.

"Correction...I'll talk with you – *soon*," he responded, then looked to the awaiting group of ladies.

"It was nice seeing all of you as well. Y'all have a good night," he said smiling. Then he resumed the walk to his car.

Everett's high was coming down. Their time together had ended sooner than he would have liked. He looked back once more to see her leave with her friends. He liked her. This he knew for certain, and he sensed that she liked him, too. Although, he imagined he'd first have to overcome a couple of hurdles in order to seal the deal. For starters, he had to make sure he wasn't moving in on Kenyan's territory. Then, he needed to figure out a way to circumvent his storied past with Samaya's sorority sisters.

Chapter 3

The advance

"Hello," spoke a voice.

The speaker didn't sound like Samaya. *It must be her roommate*, he thought.

"May I speak to Samaya?" he said.

"May I ask whose calling?" the voice returned.

"Yes, can you tell her it's Everett?"

"Hold on -- I'll see if she's available." Everett envisioned Samaya's roommate holding her hand over the phone and whispering with enthusiasm that he was on the line. He wanted Samaya to be eagerly awaiting his call because he had withheld calling her sooner. He had been anxiously waiting for this moment since bumping into her on campus less than 48 hours earlier.

"Hello."

"Hey, Miss Lady. What's up?" He asked, hoping to come across as cool and casual as possible.

"Oh, nothing much...just a little studying."

"Well, would you like me to call you back at a later time?" he asked. As bad as he wanted to talk to her, he didn't want to impose.

"No, actually you have pretty good timing; I was just about to take a break." "Cool.   I've   actually   been

looking forward to talking to you since I got back in town."
Everett decided to try a different approach since he really
wanted this girl. He figured if he avoided as many games
as possible and was forthright, his honesty and true nature
would win her over.

"So I was wondering, with you graduating in the
spring, have you given any thought as to where you want
to go after graduation? Graduation day will be here before
you know it." He figured this was a good segue into
inviting her to Atlanta for a visit.

"To be honest, I've thought a lot about Atlanta. I
hear there are a lot of good employment opportunities
there and I really don't want to live in Jacksonville. I
could be fine with just visiting my family."

Everett could not believe his ears. Things seemed
to be falling right into his lap. *It must be a sign*, he
thought.

"That's great. I think you'd like it here. Atlanta is
an absolutely wonderful place to live. The cost of living
isn't too high, and culturally, the city has a lot to offer."

"That's what I hear. One of my big sisters lives
there also."

"Who's that? I haven't run into too many people
from UF since I've been here."

"Jocelyn Trenton -- you know her, don't you?"
Not that chick...I can't stand her.

"Yeah, I know Jocelyn," he said unenthusiastically.
"She is cool with some of my "boyz," but she and I never hit
it off that well."

"She's really good people. If you got to know her,
you'd like her a lot."

Don't count on it. Everett knew all he wanted to
know about Jocelyn. She may have been cute -- even fine --
but he didn't like her attitude. She acted as if dudes were
supposed to be "all up on her." Everett did not agree. He

intentionally snubbed his nose at her. Jocelyn, in turn, showed immediate disdain for him. So, despite having mutual acquaintances, they never befriended one another.

"I'm not sure if that is going to happen, but if it helps, I sure do like you."

"Aww, that's a sweet thing to say. I like you too."

"Good. So, when can I see you again."

"You don't waste any time, do you?"

"Well, I'd just like to get to know you better, and I figured the best way to do that would be to spend some time with you."

"You might have a point there. Considering we spent two years on campus together, I know very little about you other than what I hear from my sorors. "

Damn...and things were going so well. Everett didn't know if this was a good or bad omen, but he was determined to roll with the punches. "So, just what did they tell you about me?"

"Oh, nothing bad. They said you were a pretty nice guy."

He was both surprised and relieved. He was still a bit paranoid considering the "ho" tag he had been handed a few years back. Even after lying low, he imagined that there was still some major dirt in the rumor mill about him; maybe, the dirt had finally settled.

"That's good to know. I've always thought of myself as a good guy. So, what's the real story? Why hasn't anyone snatched you up?

"Sometimes, I ask myself the same thing. Believe it or not, I haven't had a boyfriend my entire time at UF. I've gone out with a few guys, but it never seemed to go anywhere. "

"Well, I'll have to see if I can do something about that. I think we can definitely go places. My only hesitation is Kenyan, to be honest."

"Well, you need not worry about him; we're just friends."

"In your mind, you two are friends, but it's possible he could think something totally different. So...one of us needs to talk to him. If you give me his number, I'll do it." He didn't really want to call, but he was trying to be a man about it.

"I can give you his number, but -- if you like -- the next time I talk to him, I'll mention it. I really don't think it will be that big of a deal."

"You do that, and then let me know," he said, figuring she was the better person to do the talking in the first place. He didn't know the depth of their relationship, whether they had been intimate or not, and he didn't want to know. The way he saw it, the less he knew -- the better.

Their conversation went on for what seemed like hours. They joked, laughed and covered a lot of ground. They even talked about his storied past and how he put it all behind him. He didn't want her to hear it from anyone else. Everett the "playa" was no more. This man, the one she was coming to know, promised not to be perfect -- but he would be true.

Needless to say, that initial phone conversation led to a string of others that spread over the next couple of weeks. They found they had a lot of things in common and seemed to be a perfect fit. Eventually, Samaya agreed to come visit him in Atlanta. He was so excited. He felt he had found the woman of his dreams. Thanks to Samaya, Everett was living at an all-time high.

Chapter 4

The Doorway to Love

Everett couldn't believe the day had finally arrived. She was due in town by 2pm, just in time for him to finish preparing for their weekend of fun-filled surprises. It had been weeks since he saw her in Gainesville, but he made it a point to talk to her nearly every other day. He felt as if he had known her all of his life. Seeing her now would be nothing short of divine. He would have her for two full days and he wanted it to be as unforgettable as possible. He even went to the trouble of adding some decorative items to his apartment; a framed piece of art, a centerpiece for his dinette set and the latest issues of *Black Enterprise, Essence, Ebony, Jazziz* and *US News and World Report*. He wanted to fill her up with the man he was now. He wanted her to see the Everett that no other woman at UF had the pleasure of seeing.

Everything was ready to go. His apartment was cleaned as if a maid service had been there. The main living area smelled of jasmine incense and the bathroom of fresh potpourri. He even had new towels and linen ready for her visit. Nothing would spoil this weekend. This would be the official beginning to the rest of his life.

When the knock at the door came, Everett had a mix-tape playing. Dianne Reeves' sultry voice emanated throughout his one-bedroom apartment as *"Chan's Song"* played. He had taken the time to compile several tapes for the weekend so that he could impress her with his range of musical tastes; he had jazz, hip-hop, pop and R&B tapes prepared for her ears' pleasure. No matter what she was in the mood for, he was ready to satisfy her musical appetite.

"Hi!" he said, opening the door. He opened his arms to greet her. She flashed a dimpled smile and accepted his embrace. "I see you made it right on schedule," he said following a kiss to her cheek.

She walked into the one-bedroom apartment and scanned the surroundings. There was no foyer so as she stepped in from the hall into the living space. After a few short paces, she entered the dining area that contained a glass, wood and wicker dining set. The table displayed a cylindrical metal vase containing eucalyptus spray and bamboo shoots, purchased just for her visit. On the adjacent wall, to the left of the table, hung his new print *Double Dare* by Varnette P. Honeywood. Most guys his age were not hip to the artist, and they surely were not purchasing art; but Everett knew she would be impressed. When he made the purchase, he imagined her thinking that the print was like something you could see on *The Cosby Show*, which was as ceremonial as him wearing one of those fly sweaters Bill Cosby donned (but a lot cheaper in this case). Either way, it was money well spent, since Samaya seemed to be enjoying the view. In fact, where she stood, she could see most of his apartment's main furnishings.

"You have a nice place here."

"Thank you. It's a little older than some of the apartments in the area, but I chose it for its character."

"Yeah, the sunken living room makes for a nice touch, and I love the view from the balcony."

"The balcony is one of my favorite spots, especially on summer nights. It's quite relaxing to sit out there. I've even spent a few nights talking to you from there, just enjoying the moonlight and you."

It may have sounded a little corny, but Everett knew women loved romance. He intended to show her that he could make up for all the love she even *thought* she missed.

"Let me show you around the rest of the place. I want you to be absolutely comfortable since this will be your spot for the next couple of days," he said as he led her down the hall toward the kitchen.

"To your right is the kitchen. It's not too big, but it's big enough for me to show off my skills. I'm quite the chef, as you will eventually find out."

Everything was in its place, not a dish or cup was in sight. The only things in plain view were the canisters on his counter for flour, sugar, rice and grains. He also displayed his white Gevalia Kaffe coffee pot and matching toaster.

"And, just to my left is the bathroom." He reached in, turned on the light, and then stepped back so she could get a glimpse.

"It smells good in here, and everything looks so nice. Who's your decorator?" Everett smiled. He took great delight in his decorative ability, and the newly purchased Alexander Julian *Colours* bathroom set had caught her eye just as he had hoped.

"I'm glad you like it; I picked it all out myself. Now, if you follow me back toward the living room, I'll show you the bedroom."

Making their way down the hall, afforded her a better view of the living room. It housed simple furnishings: a tan upholstered sofa, a cedar polyurethane coffee table, a matching cedar bookshelf containing a stereo and, on the wall, a nice piece of art above the sofa -- *Sugar Shack*, by Ernie Barnes. The piece was made famous by the show *Good Times,* where it was featured prominently in the show's credits. He had admired the piece since he was a kid and was ecstatic to find a copy of the print in an art store in the Underground Atlanta mall.

He reached the closed door just off the living room, opened the door and flipped the switch to reveal what he hoped would eventually be the centerpiece of his love nest. The room contained a well-crafted five-piece set featuring a sleigh bed, and above the bed was a piece entitled *Starry Crown* by John Biggers. He was sure she was getting the point; she had landed herself a modern-day Renaissance Man. In that regard, he proved to be a lot different than other 25-year-old males -- at least among the heterosexual crowd. The queen-sized bed displayed a comforter set that was also from the Alexander Julian *Colours* collection. The base color was navy blue; the design -- a myriad of red, blue, and green speckles dispersed throughout -- decoratively pleasing to the female eye, but masculine in presentation. All that was left to show her was the closet.

"I moved some things around in here so you could have your own space. If you give me your keys, I'll be glad to bring your bags in." She passed him the keys, and he made his way to her car.

***

Samaya's expression radiated delight as she looked around his bedroom. She reentered the living room and slowly shook her head as she admired the décor once more. "He's got pretty good taste," she said aloud. She glanced at the coffee table and looked at the magazines. She noticed that everything in the apartment was neatly and tastefully placed. She could tell he had gone to great lengths to make an impression on her. She was glad she had come to visit Everett. *Everything* looked perfect. She was ready to commence their time together. She felt their weekend would be one to remember.

Chapter 5

Love Conceived

The parade of cars heading down Boulevard was making it difficult to find parking. Grant Park was ablaze with activity as The Juneteenth Celebration was well underway. Everett and Samaya were a couple of blocks from the actual site, but they could feel the effervescence. The streets were pulsating. Hip hop and R&B collided as festival goers made their way to the park. Brothers on foot were already submerged in the deep art of macking, while sistahs were making their last minute hair and makeup modifications during the slow drive. The smell of food permeated the air, its only interruption coming from the occasional smell of weed. Samaya rode silently as she looked wide-eyed at the sea of black people sprawled throughout the urban landscape. Everett turned to look at her, admiring her sun-kissed brown skin as he watched her gazing out of the window. He knew what was happening to her. He occasionally experienced the same phenomenon, especially at major cultural events. As her eyes followed the activity all around them, her face conveyed what he knew to be true -- the magic of Atlanta was casting its spell on her.

***

When Everett opened the trunk to pull out the picnic basket and cooler he stashed prior to her arrival, Samaya finally broke her silence.

"You went through all this trouble for me -- you shouldn't have."

"You are worth every minute it took to prepare this. It's the least I can do considering you drove the five hours to see me. Trust me, it's my pleasure."

They found themselves a nice spot on the east side of the park. The grassy hills provided them the perfect perspective for the day's festivities. As Everett lay out a blanket, they made themselves comfortable and viewed the setting. Couples lay sprawled throughout the park. Kids were playing with each other and laughing as they ran between the pockets of attendees. Others sat in lawn chairs bobbing their heads to the grooves of the unknown band that was now on stage at the south end of the park. As Everett and Samaya looked westward toward the Cyclorama, they could see the various tables and tents situated along the sidewalk with the many vendors who had come to turn a profit amidst the day's proceedings.

"Are you hungry? I prepared a nice lunch for us. We have tropical fruit salad, chicken wings, macaroni noodle salad with shrimp and sun dried tomatoes, and, for dessert, red velvet cake. With the exception of the cake, I prepared everything myself. The wings are hot off the grill, prepared this morning. They're a special recipe that I borrowed from a friend. They're called buffa-lolita wings. They are sweet with a hint of Cajun spice in them. I'm sure you'll love them; everyone raves about them whenever I make them.

"Right now, I'm just speechless! Talk about making a good impression! I wouldn't know where to start. I think

I'll just enjoy the music for now. Maybe in an hour or so I'll be ready to eat, but I'll take something to drink, if you have it."

"You know I got you," he said playfully. "Since I know you don't drink, I took the liberty to pick up a few different flavors of Snapple. You can take a look and see what you like."

"Ooo, I like those. What did you do, get a private investigator to find out everything you could about me?"

"I just pay attention. I remembered it from a previous conversation. No investigator needed."

***

Their day in the park was enchanting. They grooved for hours to the sounds of George Clinton and the P-Funk All-star's, followed by Maze featuring Frankie Beverly. Everett took pleasure in watching Samaya's body move rhythmically, subtly grooving to the vintage sounds of both bands. He smiled; knowing, his choice of outing was ideal.

Later in the day, they perused the vendor's selections of t-shirts, jewelry, artwork, literature and music and Samaya picked up a gift for her father: Joe Sample's *Spellbound* CD. Everett recommended it because Joe Sample was an old school musician whose sound transcended time. To assure her that her dad would enjoy it, he offered to pay for the gift if her father did not like it. Everett held no worries; he was proud of his ear for good jazz.

As they talked, Samaya's thoughtfulness for and remarks about her father impressed Everett. He could tell they had a healthy relationship, which further explained why she was such a great catch. Everett ascertained from his experiences that women who had good relationships with their fathers were less difficult to deal with than those who did not. Not only were they less likely to be easily bedded but they respected the role of the man in the relationship much easier than women who did not have the benefit of a good father-daughter union. Samaya was easy going, low on drama, and secure enough to allow Everett the room to be the man without apology. She was exactly the type of woman Everett had hoped for, one that was sure to love and respect him. He needed no more convincing; she was the girl for him.

***

In Everett's eyes, the day could not have been improved upon. The picnic lunch, music, leisurely strolls hand in hand, and mental stimulation seemed to stand on its own. Therefore, Everett decided that making a move on Samaya would discount the genuine nature of his feelings. This would be their first time sharing space together in the same bed and he wanted to assure her that he wanted more than sex. He needed no new proverbial notch in his belt. He wanted her heart. So, after engaging in some pillow talk, he kissed her on the forehead, turned off the light, and held her in his arms as she burrowed her head into his chest. Being with her now, like this, felt sublime -- the perfect ending to a storybook day. They both went to sleep with smiles on their faces. Thus, the evening and the morning were their first day.

***

Their Sunday together had moved along pretty rapidly. After enjoying a delectable brunch at Le Peep, site-seeing most of the day riding down Peachtree and through Buckhead, visiting stores in Little Five Points, and taking in the new Angela Bassett and Lawrence Fishburne movie, *What's Love Got to Do with It,* they made their way back to his apartment. The day had run longer than anticipated but provided ample memories for her to take home. Instead of taking her to dinner elsewhere, Everett decided he would cook for her once more. Considering the drive ahead of her, he figured Samaya would be more comfortable relaxing at his place. Plus, he wanted to enjoy this final evening alone with her without the interruption of others.

"You mind if I use your phone for a couple long distance calls. I won't be long," she said.

"Not at all, help yourself; make yourself at home," he responded.

Samaya's first call was to her roommate Anita. Everett pretended not to hear all their giggling as he prepared dinner. Samaya stayed on for about five minutes before making her second call. This time, she called her parents. He watched her through the cutout above the counter that allowed him to see into the living room. He could tell from her words that her parents did not know she was in Atlanta. Everett listened as Samaya talked to her mother, father, and brother. They all seemed to have a great relationship. He wondered if they would like him. He heard her making plans to go home for a visit soon and joking about a gift. He guessed the visit must be for her dad's upcoming birthday. As he continued to pretend he was not listening, he hoped that he would get the chance to meet them one day soon.

"Sorry about being on the phone so long. I haven't talked to my parents in a while and my dad's birthday is coming up. I was joking with him about his gift, so I told him I picked him up a nice pet rock that I was sure he was going to love." Everett let out chuckle as she continued. "He and I have this tradition of buying each other gag gifts, but I always get him something nice to go along with it. I'm going to see them week after next, once all my finals are done. Then I'm going back two weeks after that for a friend's wedding. I was thinking maybe you can drive down and come with me on one of the weekends; I'd love for you to meet my parents."

"Wow, I get the invite to see the parents already. You must really like me."

Samaya blushed. "I guess you are okay; I won't kick you to the curb just yet. Besides, it smells like you know what you are doing in there. I could use a man who knows how to cook."

"I would have thought that after yesterday, you'd be convinced that I was the real deal. I told you I can get down. So tell me, what time are you planning to pull out tomorrow? Not that I'm trying to get rid of you or anything...because if it was up to me, you'd never have to leave."

"Funny you should say that. I was talking to my roommate, and I told her I was having such a good time that I was thinking about staying an extra day. Not to mention, I haven't had the chance to see Jocelyn yet, and she knows I'm in town. I was going to call her and see if we could meet up tomorrow for lunch. If it's okay with you, I could stay and get some studying done while you are at work and then leave on Tuesday morning. You wore me out with all of our activities, and I'm a little too tired to get back on the road tomorrow. So what do you think?"

"It sounds great to me! I'd love to have you here another day! Stay as long as you like!"

Samaya smiled.

"Girl, you sure have a pretty smile."

"Thank you. Your cookie eating grin isn't half bad either."

"Oh, you got jokes. But, that's cool; I'm going to let you slide this time, since you're a guest and all," he said, chuckling. "From the sounds of your earlier conversation you do a lot of joke telling. What was all that giggling about during your first phone call?" Everett asked

"Oh that was Anita, trying to get in my business, and being comical as usual. We were just having "girl talk." She's a lot of fun. She's planning a multi-night sleepover with some of our line sisters as soon as I get back. We're going to hang out at Tiffany's place and study for finals together."

"Sounds like fun."

"Yeah, we haven't gotten together like that since we were all on line, so it should be a blast."

Everett completed cooking their meal and they enjoyed the food while talking and savoring smooth R&B rhythms. When they finished eating, they washed dishes together. He washed; she dried.

***

When Everett finished his shower, he could not believe his eyes as he walked into his bedroom. Samaya sat on his bed, clad in an inviting piece of red lingerie.

"Play something nice for me," she said.

"I have just what the doctor ordered. I'll be right back."

Everett walked into the living room and picked out the mix-tape that he was holding for this special moment. He could barely contain his joy. He wanted to jump in the air and say, "Yeah!" but he played it cool. Returned to the bedroom and lit the candles sitting on his dresser. Turning down the lights to allow the candlelight to dance while also creating just the right level of ambience, Everett removed his robe so that only his torso was exposed, leaving nothing but his Polo lounging pants covering everything below. He put in the tape and pressed *Play*. Samaya looked on seductively in silence.

"I've got another surprise for you," he said, in a low husky voice.

"And just what would that be?" she responded in kind.

As soon as the last syllable escaped her lips, she heard the opening track, *"Kissing You"* by Keith Washington. Everett began to serenade her.

As he sang, Everett made his way to the bed. "Lie down," he whispered. She complied, moving from her upright position to a supine perspective. He positioned himself next to her and while looking into her eyes, began kissing her softly to the music: *Kissing you/Loving you all through the night/Share my love/Tonight is our night, together, yeah...*

She was reserved but consenting. Everett was likely one of few men that she had ever been with. That thought sobered him slightly, so he took things slowly; he did not want to overwhelm her, since he had plans to take his time. While kissing her, he slid her camisole up and began kissing her awakened nipples. He liked the feel of her body, nice and athletically taut. But, as he slid his hands lower he worried that he might still be moving too fast, so he avoided freeing her of her undergarments. He wanted to make sure they arrived at the apex at the exact same moment; he wanted to be the best she ever had. Foreplay, he decided was what he needed to concentrate on -- more blowing, nibbling, sucking, licking and caressing -- because a woman *did not* like to be rushed when the sex was good. He wanted her to be comfortable with him; that required him to give into her body's beckoning while forsaking his desire for immediacy. Give her all the time she needed to become familiar with the feel, taste and smell of him. Tonight, like the whole weekend, was all about her and conveying what he felt for her through his actions. He wanted her to feel the words that he was hesitant to say. He wanted to show her that he loved her.

***

The previous night had been wonderful. Everett woke early to make sure Samaya would be fine in the house and city alone. The first order of business was breakfast. He prepared a variety of items not knowing exactly what she would want; eggs, cheese grits, toast, salmon patties and bacon. He knew she wouldn't eat it all, but he did not care. He just wanted to cater to her while she was there.

"I didn't know what you would like to eat, but this should work for starters. If you don't like any of this, I have some Golden Grahams and Frosted Flakes in the cabinet."

"No! This is fine. Thank you. You really know how to make a sister feel appreciated. As if last night wasn't enough, I wake up to this. You are some kinda special, Mr. Goins."

"I guess you bring out the best in me. What can I say? You are a queen. I wouldn't feel right treating you any other way. I'm just glad you decided to stay another day. I definitely wasn't ready for you to leave. I wish I had known ahead of time because I would have taken off. Our office really get's hit when one person decides not to show, so I need to go in, but it sure is tempting."

"Don't worry about it. I'm going to get a head start on studying. Then I'm going to meet Jocelyn for lunch and hang out with her for a few hours. Speaking of which, I need to get directions from you so I can get to her job."

"Not a problem. You go ahead and eat while I finish preparing for work." He kissed her on the forehead.

"You know it's really good having you here," he said as he walked off.

Everett wanted to tell her he loved her, but felt maybe it was too soon. He knew she liked him, but he did not want to scare her by coming on so strong. He would tell her soon, once he knew she was totally cool with the ideas floating around in his head. He was already seeing Samaya and he married and living in Atlanta.

***

Samaya was in heaven. Everett was everything she had heard and more. Not only was he an excellent lover, but he was also a gentleman. She could not wait to talk to her girls to tell them about all the nice things he had done for and to her while she was visiting. She could still smell his scent. *What a wonderful man he is,* she thought. She smiled as she recalled the previous night's encounter. *I'm going to have to get some more of that before I leave,* she thought. She had never felt like this about any guy, with the exception of Kenyan, but she did not want to think of him at a time like this; Everett had her attention. If he played his cards right, she would definitely be moving to Atlanta after graduation.

Her parents had set aside six months worth of expenses to assist her with her post graduation transition. She was sure she could find a job; she just wanted to be near him. He was the type of guy she could see herself happily married to. She wondered what her girls would think about that. They told her just to come and have a good time, and not to expect too much, too soon. Everett was a nice guy, they said, but he had broken a few hearts in his day. She would have to be careful. She would need to play it safe. Samaya did not get that feeling about him. He was so open and easy to talk to. All those nights on the phone convinced her that he must have been a different guy back then because the Everett she knew was not a heartbreaker; he was proving to be the man she wanted to give her heart. And, as much as she would hate to admit to her girls, she was already falling in love. *Everett and Samaya, hmm, that has a nice ring to it.*

***

Everett's alarm clock went off way too soon. She would be leaving today. As the awareness of that fact began to wear in, he started to miss her. He could not believe the way she made him feel. His nose was wide open. There was no denying it; he was in love. He looked at her lying next to him and he wanted to give her another taste of last night's lovemaking session. *"I better not,"* he thought. *"She has a long drive ahead of her."*

As she slowly awakened, she fixated on his image and was greeted by his words.

"Good morning."

"Good morning," she replied with a smile.

"How'd you sleep?"

"Thanks to you, very well. I guess you could say that I slept like a baby. I feel like I'm ready for the road now."

"I wish you didn't have to go," he said as he made puppy-dog eyes at her.

"Me either, but those classes are calling. I think I'll shower and get some food on the road. I want to get back at a decent time."

"Yeah, I better get up and start ironing my clothes. No sense in dragging my morning out. But I can't say it enough -- I'm sure going to miss you."

"Awww, I'm going to miss you too, but you'll see me in a couple of weeks when you go home with me. You should be able to manage until then. Besides, we still can talk to each other by phone."

Chapter 6

Everett could not understand why she had not called. He figured she had made it home by at least three o'clock yesterday. Although he was still at work when she arrived home, he could not imagine why she didn't at least leave him a message. He had left her a couple messages last night and another this morning. The least she could do was return his calls. It was making it hard for him to concentrate at work. He scrolled through his mind to see if he overlooked something she told him that would explain her not calling. He remembered her telling him about the sleepover at Tiffany's place. He was sure that was going well. They probably wanted every little detail from her weekend. He hoped they would all be jealous and wish they had taken a second look at him. But considering she had not called, maybe they were laughing at him. Maybe, this was all a little game they were playing on him. Maybe, she didn't like him at all and this was some twisted game her sorors put her up to. *Nah, that couldn't be it.* As much game as he had run in his day, there was no way he could have gotten suckered like that. Not by her.

Something was wrong. He could feel it in the pit of his stomach. He left the car rental counter and walked to the back office to make the call. After several rings, he got her voicemail again. "Hi, this is Samaya, leave a message." The beep was really long this time. This was only his fourth call. He wondered who else had left her messages. Maybe they had accumulated over the weekend, but he did not remember the beep being that long this morning when he called. "Dang," he heard himself say aloud, "I need to call someone else." He thought long and hard about who he could call. He realized he did not have anyone's number that knew her. Then, his mind landed on Jocelyn. He recalled the directions he gave Samaya and remembered that Jocelyn worked for Bally's on La Vista Road.

"Bally's Health and Fitness, can I help you please?" asked the voice on the other end of the line.

"May I speak to Jocelyn Trenton please?"

"Sure, hold one moment."

Everett tapped his fingers impatiently on the counter, trying to gather his next words.

"Jocelyn speaking, how may I help you?"

"Jocelyn, this is Everett -- Everett Goins. Sorry to bother you at work, but I haven't heard from Samaya since she left and I was wondering if you had a number I could reach her at."

She did not respond right away. She paused just long enough for him to suspect something. "Everett...I don't know how to tell you this, but...Samaya died in a car accident on the way back to Gainesville."

No! He closed his eyes upon hearing her words. *Not Samaya.* "Is this some joke! You've got to be kidding me. There must be some mistake!" he heard himself say. He could not believe his ears. His mind went blank. The surprise of her words had staggered him.

"Everett, I'm sorry," she said. He could hear her tears. *This was actually real --*

How? When? Where did it happen? He had questions, but nothing would come out. The thoughts were just colliding in his mind.

"I don't believe it. I just saw her. I was supposed to go see her in a couple of weeks, I lov---," he said as he went from silence to rambling, not really talking to Jocelyn, just speaking audible thoughts.

He searched for words to say...but found none.

"Hey...umm, I need to get back to the floor, but would you like me to call you when I have information regarding the services?"

He slowly took in her words as if they were being typed out for him. He ran them over in his mind again and realized he needed to respond. "Umm, yes, that will be fine. I can't believe this is happening," he muttered.

"I know. Everyone is torn up over this. She meant a lot to all of us." She paused, and then spoke again. "Can I get your number real quick?"

"Oh, I'm sorry. Umm...my number is...umm...404-698-2375, my work number is 770- 465-5306; please call me as soon as you know something. I definitely want to pay my respects."

"I sure will. You'll definitely hear back from me. You take care." Everett lowered the phone from his ear. He could not apprehend what had just happened. This could not be. He picked up the phone again and dialed Samaya's number again. The recorder picked up. He closed his eyes while listening to her voice and tried to picture her. This all seemed so surreal. There was no need to leave a message...the machine was full. It was the fifth time he heard her voice since she left. He had not imagined it would be his last.

Chapter 7

Everett never anticipated meeting Samaya's parents like this. He could not believe he was at her funeral, but the dark clothes, mournful expressions and familiar faces were proof enough. Students he had not seen in years were there, crying, looking for answers. Word had apparently spread that she had been in Atlanta with him and several of her sorority sisters approached him wanting to know if she died "happy." *What the hell did they mean by that?* After the second Delta approached him he figured they wanted to know if Samaya and he had sex during her visit. *The nerve of them! I aint tellin' them shit! They should have been ashamed of themselves to even broach the subject. She was dead for God's sake.*

Everett's surprise of the day came when Kenyan walked in the door of the chapel. He was with several of his frat brothers. Everett knew that word would eventually get to Kenyan that Samaya was with him before her death -- if it had not already reached him. This was the first time in their friendship that he wanted to avoid Kenyan. He was not sure if Samaya had the talk with him about their budding relationship, and it was certainly too late to explain now. Since they were "boyz," he had to say something. When their eyes met Everett's stomach went into a freefall. Not a good sign. This was exactly what he tried to avoid in the first place -- a confrontation. Now, it was inevitable. Samaya was gone, and he had to explain how they had come to be a couple.

Everett made his way over to where Kenyan was standing.

"Can I talk to you for a minute...in private?" Kenyan did not respond. He just motioned with his hand for Everett to lead the way. They exited the chapel and went into the parking lot, stopping amidst the parked cars and away from the flow of foot traffic.

"Yeah, what's up?" he said flatly.

Everett let out a sigh. "I'm not sure if you know, but Samaya came to see me this past weekend."

"Yeah, she told me."

Everett was relieved to hear that, but it still did not make it easy to talk to his friend under these circumstances.

"Man, I just want you to know I really cared about her a lot. She wasn't just something I was doing," Everett was trying to make things right. Kenyan's body language spoke his dissatisfaction; he did not have to say a word. Everett talked some more to limit the dead space hoping that would help clear his conscious.

"In fact, we talked about you. I told her I didn't want to start dating her if it wasn't cool with you."

"So what do you expect me to say? That it was cool?" Kenyan's remark was devoid of affection. "I know you remember my telling you specifically that she was the kind of girl you marry. The kind of girl *I wanted to marry!*" He said, raising his voice.

Dang, I can't believe he remembered those words too.

"Look man, it wasn't planned. I just sort of stumbled up on her. What did you expect me to do?"

"You could have been a friend and stepped off," Kenyan said, clearly not masking his feelings.

There was more silence. This time it was the uncomfortable kind.

"You know what? I have no one to blame but myself. I had every opportunity to be with Samaya. I'm just mad at you because you did what I wasn't willing to do. If not you, it would have been someone else. She was a good girl; someone was bound to scoop her up eventually."

Everett wanted to speak. He wanted to concur with what Kenyan was saying, but he opted for silence and let Kenyan continue talking. "Look man, it's cool. More than anything, Samaya and I were friends, so we did talk about the two of you. I realized you weren't just trying to mack her, and I could tell she liked you a lot; so I didn't want to stand in the way of that. I didn't like it, but I cared enough about her not to be selfish."

Everett was astonished and relieved at the same time. He did not know what to say.

"Wow. Thanks, man. She told me she would talk to you, but I never got the opportunity to find out if she had. I really dug her man. She was really special."

Kenyan just shook his head knowingly.

"Well, I'm not going to keep you. We can get up later, cool?" Everett asked.

"Cool," Kenyan responded. They gave each other "dap," and as they came in for the embrace, Kenyan spoke quietly in Everett's ear, "On second thought, I can't let you off that easy. You know the rules. Unhh!" Kenyan grunted, as he stuck Everett with a sharp fist into his right side. Everett folded into the blow and slumped down to ease the pain. Looking down at him, Kenyan said, "You deserved that one. Now we can be cool"

Everett winced, caught his breath, and then nodded from his slumped position. "Alright, I'll take that. You're right; I deserved that one."

***

As Everett sat in the back of the chapel, all the activity around him faded into white noise. He was back in the park with her, watching her as he lay on the blanket they were sharing. He remembered how peaceful she looked as she watched Frankie Beverly and Maze perform. Samaya was indeed a "southern girl;" so sweet, loving and kind. The more he thought about that moment in the park, the more he wondered if she somehow knew in her spirit that these were her last days on earth. He remembered her state of tranquility as she sat with her legs pulled into her chest, shades over her eyes, and arms folded and resting at the top of her knees. He recalled thinking that she was really savoring the feeling of that warm June day. He wished he could share another of those moments with her. Wished he could turn back the clock and date her in college. Wished he could have been there to save her. He wished an innumerable amount of scenarios that would allow them to still remain together. As he sat there thinking of her, the tears began rolling down his cheek. He did not want to let her go. She was his dream come true. She was the woman he had waited so long for; she was...one to remember.

The End

worlds apart

they say with God anything is possible
so now i scar my knees
in search of his loving kindness
His tender mercy
my heart asks for forgiveness for my needless acts of sin
i desire to make amends but how do i begin
where do i begin
when

no one knows my heart
no one knows my soul
my mind speaks of the greatest romance ever told
but in order to give
another has to know how as well as be able to receive
one has to be willing to believe
in the presence
the essence

just once i would love to capture that abundant feeling
with everything inside of me
make it last
so often we tend to think back to that moment in time once the
feelings have passed
but does the belief have to pass
why can't the sentiment last forever
just as a breath of fresh air or a dozen roses to show someone
cares
there are instances which remain priceless
in so many ways I was lifeless
until our paths crossed
only time will tell whether my direction remains lost

knowing is half the battle they say
I am thankful you have come my way
I am not asking you to hold my hand

but please understand how I am reaching out to you the only
way I can
from my heart
even though we are worlds apart
tis' true
there is a great distance which lies between me and you
the difference between night and day
during our conversations somehow I do not feel that way

I feel blessed yet so unworthy it seems
and I say that while being unaware of any problem with my self
esteem
I have seen what my world had to offer
not exactly food for the soul
I believe I can fly no matter what I was told
faith weak
desire remained strong
even when I was right a part of me always felt I was wrong
until you came along

they say if God brings you to it
He shall lead you through it
I never learned how to hold my head and simply do it
I would always go through it
through the fire
but my friendship with you has given me a newfound desire
my precious friend this much is true
although we are worlds apart I believe in my heart
I would cross the stars for you

Donald Smith

Dedication

This tale is dedicated to the grandfather I never knew. Rest In peace brother.

THE MENDING
A Soldier's Tale
By D.R. Johnson

"In other news, the President has announced that there will soon be a handing over of power, and a scaling back of troop strength in the recently established "New Democratic Iraq." Opponents of his plan have made it clear that to leave now will further jeopardize American interests in the region, and that staying the course is the only option..." announced the news correspondent in a carefully measured pentameter that pecked at the edge of Abe Deaks' patience.

"Hazel, turn that damn T.V. off! You know I can't hardly stand to listen to it anymore" he grumbled.

"Sorry," she sighed. "It's just, you know, Jarl is supposed to be here tomorrow, and... this wouldn't be the first time he's told us he'd be coming home, and then have his release date pushed back" lamented Hazel with obvious frustration and concern.

"Will you relax with all that? The boy was there for a good reason. He's protectin' his country, *our* country from those terrorists" retorted Abe.

"Yeah, I know Abe, but I just wonder if it's worth it... I mean, so much killing... and for what? Oil?"

"We've been over this so many times woman! It's not about oil, it's about keepin' us safe from gettin' blown up. You saw those towers fall same as me...it's our way of life that's under attack, and they're not goin' to stop until we're all dead. Meanin' it's us, or them. Our boy has been over there riskin' his neck to make sure we are OK back here! At least respect that enough to stop complainin' about it for once."

Abe was right about one thing, thought Hazel, *the two of them ·had been through this same conversation many times over*. In fact, it seemed to her that Abe never actually listened to anything she said to him about the war. At times his selected deafness was unbearable, but that was just Abe. When he made up his mind on a thing, there was no changing it, and she had learned to live with this aspect of his personality long ago. Despite her quiet resignation to bite her tongue, there was a part of her that could not help but blame Abe for their son's enlistment. Maybe if he hadn't spent so much time filling the boy's ears with star spangled histrionics, maybe if he hadn't spent so much time spouting off about the Holy War... just maybe her boy would have left well enough alone instead of rushing head long into that damnable war.

***

The Deaks lived in a small town in Southern Iowa, typical in many ways of most small American towns, having sprung up around farming, and eventually losing out to the push for modernization. There existed a strange dichotomy between old and new as large parcels of land were being sold off to accommodate the ever growing urban sprawl. The wealthy clamored to leave the big cities, and with them they brought their money, their neighborhoods, and their culture. Although the Five and Dime still stood on Main street, and farmers still gathered at the Plow & Feed to spend their Saturday afternoons chewing the fat, life had changed dramatically for their small town. Many businesses found it impossible to compete with Shop Rite's prices, and McDonald's speed, and in one generations time they had seen the landscape of their community drastically altered. While some folks frowned upon this strange marriage of modern money versus meager means, others viewed it as a blessing. To the newer residents of the little town, life represented an escape from the hustle & bustle of a nine to five, a reprieve from the smog, a chance to pretend all was right in the world. Yet for the younger generation, growing up here seemed devoid of potential with very few options. Sure there were plenty of opportunities to be had in town if you didn't mind stocking shelves or flipping burgers, but aside from that the choice was farm, or find work elsewhere.

Jarl Deaks was among those who had grown up wanting to see the world beyond small town life, and visit those far off places he'd seen on television. He wanted to attend college, but his parents had made it clear that there was absolutely no way they could afford to pay for his schooling, and that he'd be much better off if he would set his goals to something more attainable, like helping out on the farm. However, this request would prove next to impossible for the boy. Jarl was a dreamer, and not a day passed by in which his father hadn't felt it necessary to chide him with timeworn phrases like 'take your head out of the clouds,' 'think before you act,' and 'be mindful of your responsibilities'. Whether or not this had any influence over the boy's state of mind, one thing was for certain, he could not stop dreaming about his future elsewhere anymore than he could force himself to want to follow in his father's footsteps and carry on the family farm. Life for Jarl was not about tractors, or praying that the corn would be knee high by July. For Jarl there was more to life than could be had in a small rural town, and this presented itself as quite a dilemma for the lad, because it seemed to him that there was no way out.

Then along came that tragic fate filled day that no one living in America would ever be able to erase from their memory. The nation stood still, as people everywhere gathered around their radios and television sets staring in shock as hijacked airliners rained down, crashing one after the other into the twin towers of the World Trade Center, and then into the Pentagon. They stood gaping in horror as the people who found themselves stranded in the upper levels of the towers hurled themselves out of windows to avoid being burned alive. As the towers collapsed, Americans sat and watched New York City as it was enveloped in a heavy blanket of ash and the fires spread. Buildings collapsed one into another like dominos, throwing the metropolis into a panic with no end to the chaos in sight. Days later, Americans continued to watch as the rescue workers with their cranes and dump trucks cleared away millions of tons of debris. They grimaced, sick to their stomachs whenever a firefighter removed a wristwatch, or someone's wallet from beneath the piles of rubble and debris. They waited anxiously to hear each updated death toll, magnifying every report in their own minds a hundred fold. The U.S. government was quick to place blame. 'We believe those responsible for the attacks on September the eleventh are members of an Islamic terrorist organization known as Al-Qaeda' was the official line that played non-stop over the cable news circuit. In the midst of elevated "terrorist threat levels" Americans rushed out and bought guns in record number, and the red white and blue could be seen flying at nearly every house, on every street in America.

It was shortly after that gruesome chain of events,

that the recruiters began appearing at every small town high school around the country, hoping to take advantage of a reinvigorated sense of national unity and patriotism. They preyed upon young men like Jarl, imploring them to 'serve their country' and to 'be all that they could be.' The National Guard recruiters made it sound like the American way of life was under attack, and able bodied young people were needed to protect her stateside, while the "active" branches of the military sped to defend her in the Middle East. What they failed to mention was that for the first time in American history, reservists and guardsmen would be called up to active duty on a massive scale, to mobilize and deploy indefinitely overseas. And so it was, amidst his mother's constant pleas, and his father's daily diatribes on Islam's hatred of all things American, Jarl signed on the dotted line, offering up four years of his young life in service of his country.

***

As he stared out through the stains that covered the window, Jarl's thoughts lingered back to his life before the war. It had been 1,433 days since he'd last seen his home, and the irony was not lost on him that now, with only twenty-seven days left in his contract with Uncle Sam, he was being allowed leave. As he pondered this, he wondered if he would ever reach a point in his life that he could stop counting the days. It was like counting sheep when trying to fall asleep, only Jarl was trying to wake up. --One-- suicide bomber,--two-- snipers on the roof,--three-- dead friends. As the old Greyhound rolled down the highway, his thoughts turned to who might be waiting at the farm to welcome him home, and he caught himself hoping there would be no one. The last thing he felt like doing was explaining himself to a group of people who hadn't a clue. He dreaded the questions that were sure to be asked. "How many of those terrorists did you kill Jarlie?" he imagined his Grandpa asking. Next would come the capricious chirping of his nephews; "Yeah, tell us about some of your battles... did you bring home your gun; can we see it!?"

The road stretched onward much further than his eye could see, with row after row of cornfield breaking up an otherwise featureless landscape save for the random barn here, or windmill there. Still, Jarl knew exactly where he was just as surely as if he were in his own backyard, and in a way that is precisely where he was. It had been awhile since he'd last seen this part of the state, and recollections of passing through on family vacations swirled about his memory as if it were only yesterday. His life had seemed so simple back then, never having to worry about anything beyond his latest puppy love, or scraping together enough cash to buy next month's comic books. He remembered how badly he wanted a driver's license, and when he finally got it how dejected he'd felt on realizing first hand the cost of gas. *What a terrible fool he'd been to believe he could make a difference*, Jarl mused. He'd have done better to have stayed home and spent an eternity flipping burgers, than to have sold his soul to the war machine. Somewhere in the bottom of Jarl's leathery heart there still lived an innocent child unchanged by his experiences, but those moments when he felt carefree and alive had become few and far between. More often, the man felt certain the child was long dead. He felt old, far too old, and as the regret washed over him, Jarl felt that familiar drowning sensation that usually indicated he was slipping into a dream. As he peered out across the cornfields, he drifted off into a fitful sleep that lasted the remainder of his journey. Asleep, Jarl did not notice as the bus, belching exhaust and reeking of road, lumbered into the parking lot of the old brick station.

Several minutes after all the other passengers had exited the bus, the driver walked back to where Jarl was sitting, and upon seeing that he had dozed off, gently placed his hand against the young man's shoulder, jostling him slightly.

"Excuse me sir," he ventured "but we're here, I believe this is your destination."

This was enough to startle Jarl into consciousness, and he bolted upright. A cold sweat covered his brow as he glanced about in confusion through half closed eyes. Instinctively, frantically, he began probing the seat next to him with his hand, feeling around for his gun. Around the time he realized that there was no gun, his eyes had adjusted themselves to the light just enough that he could make out the orange interior of the vehicle, and the expression of the driver standing next to him. He glowered up at the man with a look that seemed to convey both anger and embarrassment.

"I-I'm sorry sir, I didn't mean to startle you" stammered the driver, "say, is everything OK? You don't look so good..." and just as he was about to take a defensive step backwards, seemingly to his great relief, Jarl's expression softened into a look of weary sadness, and his fists unclenched. The driver heaved a sigh of relief as Jarl slowly stood up and went about gathering his gear. Without saying a word, Jarl brushed past the man, and headed towards the door. As he stepped down out of the gas guzzling giant, he peered around, squinting against the glare of the setting Sun, and discovered that only his father was there to pick him up.

On seeing his son exit the bus, Abe somewhat stiff and deliberately rose up into a standing position, and then waddled towards his son like an old bulldog in cowboy boots. The two men's eyes met, and Abe, overcome with emotion could not hold it in a second more, "Well I'll be! There he is. Aren't you a sight for sore eyes Jarlie boy!?"

"Hey dad" returned Jarl, pretending to smile.

"Let me get a look at you boy" bellowed Abe, grasping

both of Jarl's arms just below the shoulder with his heavy work worn hands. Abe's eyes seemed to scrutinize the young man, like a prospector, analyzing every crevice for some sign or hidden quality.

"What they been feedin' you over there? You look half starved."

"The standard chow dad, cardboard and dust, a lot of field rations, you know how it is."

Abe eyed the boy skeptically after this statement.

"Must be more to it then that Jarlie. Remember who you're talkin' to here, I've known you your whole life...besides, I did my time in Korea and I don't remember seein' anyone lookin' like you do now on account of the food bein' bad!"

"Well, I don't know dad...might be due to stress. Least that's what the shrink told me before approving my leave. Said they were evaluating us all for post traumatic stress something or other." Jarl was careful not to mention the nightmares he'd been suffering from. There might be a time and place for that discussion, but the bus station was not it.

"Stress huh? Well never mind any of that quack's mumbo jumbo, when I finished up my last tour, they gave us a swift kick in the behind and told us to have a nice life. Besides, the Deaks are made of tougher stuff then that. Listen here though, mind you don't bring that up when you see your mom, she's been sick with worry these last few months. Abe put his arm around Jarl's shoulders. Giving him a squeeze, he pointed over to where he had parked his pick-up.

"C'mon son, I got the truck parked right over there, let's get you home."

The Dodge seemed older, rustier than Jarl remembered, but then again, maybe it just seemed that way in the dull glow of the Sun as it tucked in behind the horizon. Jarl peered out across the fields, and the feeling that stared back chilled him to the marrow. Where was the elation, the joy he imagined he would experience being back home? This was not his home anymore. The corn fields in their green, pungent majesty were equally as foreign to his senses as the parched desert where he had once been. After driving several miles in silence, Abe decided to try and break the ice with idle conversation.

"So how about it son, did you kill any of those A-rabs while you were over there?"

"Yeah dad, I did, and I'm not proud to say it either."

"What do you mean you're 'not proud to say it?'" asked Abe, as his face turned bright red, "they come over here, threatenin' our freedom, killin' thousands of poor innocent people, and you tell me you're not proud that you took the fight to their doorstep?"

"Dad, please. I'd really rather not get into this with you right now. But if you really want to know, yeah, I'm ashamed of what I've done, what we've done. You say 'poor and innocent' like that's some quality exclusive to being an American... can we talk about something else for awhile?"

"Fine then, I won't ask you anymore about it, but can you blame me? I haven't seen you for over three years now." After a brief pause, Abe turned his head slightly so that he could look his son in the eye when he said what he would say next.

"You know, I couldn't be more proud of you, Jarlie. I tell everyone how you took up freedom's call and headed over to that shit hole...you know son, it's men like you and I, that through the years have made the United States of America what she is today."

Jarl was uneasy at hearing this and frowned while trying to swallow, but his throat had gone dry. He had forgotten how blindly patriotic his father could be, and it made him sick to his stomach to think that four years ago, he had been the same way himself, and look where it had gotten him.

"Yeah dad, men like you and me," murmured Jarl under his breath.

"Alright son, you don't want to talk now, I can respect that, we'll have plenty of time to catch up later." Having said that, the two men fell into a silence broken only by the occasional thump of the truck running through potholes in the road, and the random rattle and clunk of the engine.

The Sun had finished setting and the sky was dark as they pulled into the Deaks farm. Even so, Jarl squinted to see through the glare of the halogen flood lamp mounted on the front of the barn. As the truck slowed to a halt, a river of memory washed over him, its current threatening to pull him under. So much within Jarl had changed during his time spent away from this place. On the exterior he tried hard to appear as if he was the same Jarl his family and friends remembered, but inside he felt half dead. Before he could dwell on this any further, the screen door burst open with such intensity it would have been no surprise to see it come clean off its hinges. His mother dashed crossed the front porch with such speed that Jarl halfway expected her to leap over the steps and tumble headlong towards the truck. After noticing that he was still in the pick-up, he carefully opened his door, so as not to throw anything dangerous into his mother's path, as she hurtled towards him like a meteor that just broke atmosphere. Hazel Deaks, not saying a word, threw herself at the boy, giving him such a bear hug it was a wonder she didn't lift him off the ground. Clasping her hands behind his head, she began kissing him on the forehead, and fawning over him the way mothers do after their child has wandered off at the fairground or any other similarly large public place, and been lost for an excruciatingly long time. Her eyes met with his, and they spoke with a voice of their own, born of part desperation, part inspection, and mostly just raw love.

"Mom..." started Jarl.

"Shhh" she replied, "let me get a good look at you. You've come back to me a man haven't you..."

"Mom, I'm sorry I couldn't write you more, it's just that..."

"Hush now, I don't want to hear any of that. What's important is that you're back home, even if it's only for a week, you're here, and you're in one piece. Sweet Jesus, my prayers have been answered!"

Both mother and son turned their heads in unison to see Abe approaching.

"When you two are about done being mushy... I've been waiting a longtime to see the boy, and hear straight out the horses' mouth how things have been goin' over there" Abe interjected.

"Don't you ever think about anything else?" Hazel asked frustrated with her husband.

"Well it's near impossible isn't it? It's all over the radio and TV. I go up to the hardware store, and they're talking about Iraq. I stop in to the P&F, and what do you suppose they're talking about? Every Sunday the pastor figures out some fancy new way to drop the word terrorist into the sermon..." Abe said defensively, while throwing his hands up to indicate that he could go on listing examples if need be.

"Does that mean we need to talk about it all the time here? Give the child a chance to settle in, maybe we can talk about this over supper?" pleaded Hazel.

"So where is everyone?" asked Jarl, trying to change the subject. "I figured half the family would be here to see how I was doing..."

"You know how it is, they dangled that carrot in front of you so often, sayin' they'd let you take leave, then cancelin' at the last minute... I guess no one was sure if you'd really be here," Abe said contemptuously.

After a long and awkward silence, Jarl decided he'd go inside and stow his gear in his old bedroom. The room had hardly changed at all since last he'd seen it, and as he glanced about he couldn't help but reminisce on simpler times. Walking over to the closet, an old box caught his eye. Tugging at the bent and worn cardboard flap at its corner revealed the contents, and a small grin broke crossed Jarl's face as he realized what he was holding; it was his old GI-Joes. Most of them were missing their thumbs, and some were without limbs due to heavy play, but still, there they were, a tangible reminder of the boy he used to be. Thinking on how he used to play with those action figures, imagining that he would one day grow up to be like them; strong, courageous, disciplined, his smile faded. How wrong he'd been about so many things. The reality of war, just as it had with so many other memories, cast a dark shadow over another simple pleasure, stripping away the magic of innocence. Jarl let out a long sigh as he tried to juxtapose his childhood fantasies of battle with his actual experiences, and just ended up further illustrating in vivid detail how foolish he'd been. War had nothing to do with codenames or ninjas, there were no laser guns set to stun, no miraculous vehicles that could transform from one thing to another... just fear, hatred and death. Realizing how exhausted he felt from the jet lag, Jarl lay back on the bed and as he stared at the ceiling drifted off into a fitful sleep.

The dreamscape he found himself in had established itself as an increasingly familiar scene. He always knew that he was dreaming because he had been there so many times before. Yet despite this awareness of where he was, and what was happening, he was at the mercy of his unconscious mind, unable to conquer the situation or resolve it, and it was beginning to feel like every time he closed his eyes, this scene played itself out. The true horror of it was rooted in the fact that this dream bore a disturbing similarity to an actual experience he had been involved with while stationed in Iraq. Worse still, was the knowledge Jarl held while asleep, that this pivotal event revealed his own failings, and the frail preciousness of life. Try as he might, the dream was never carried over into his waking reality allowing for analysis, and after many evenings fraught with turmoil Jarl was still unable to conquer his fears. And therefore, as it had on so many previous occasions, the dream stole in taking hold of Jarl's soul and tightened it's ever present metaphysical noose.

And so, the dream played itself out in his mind as it had hundreds of times prior, one more time. It was late in the evening, and his company was on a routine patrol searching door to door for insurgents that had been reported in and around the neighborhood. As they entered people's homes, Jarl was taken aback by the fury in their eyes, and the severity of their scowls. Each house seemed the same as the last. Windows shattered by gunfire, no electricity, and sparsely furnished with at least half a dozen women and children huddled with their backs to the walls, desperately pleading in a language he couldn't understand that the lives of their children be spared. This patrol was to be done by the numbers; they couldn't afford to make any mistakes. Several soldiers had been wounded, and another killed just last week on a standard patrol, and this weighed heavily on the soldier's minds. As they swept through the house, they lifted rugs searching for trap doors, and tapped the butt ends of their weapons against suspicious looking sections of wall that seemed like they might be hiding a crawl space, or some other means by which an enemy combatant could hide. Just as they were preparing to leave, all hell broke loose. The house erupted in shouting and screaming. A disheveled young man, face obscured below the nose by a white cloth, barely large enough to cover his beard, burst into the common room. He had chosen to shield himself with a young girl, who despite her struggles was unable to wrench free of the man's arm held over her neck. The man rapidly alternated between pointing the gun at her head, and then his own, and then back to hers, indicating his willingness to kill, and complete disrespect for her life as well as his own.

The translator in their group took a step forward with his hands raised, showing the assailant that he held no weapon and he just wanted to talk. After a heated exchange in Arabic containing what seemed to Jarl much cursing, the translator turned back towards the soldiers saying "he intends to kill the little girl if we do not offer him safe passage from this house."

"Gee, you think?" scoffed one of the soldiers standing next to Jarl.

"Screw that," shouted another, "he don't make the terms, we do!"

Pressing the gun hard against the girls head, the man in the mask indicated that he was ready and willing to pull the trigger.

"Damn it, say something" Jarl pleaded, looking over at the translator.

The translator, with a hint of desperation in his tone, begged the man once again in Arabic to comply. The man shook his head violently and let out a deeply tormented hissing sound.

"Forget this," grunted the soldier standing beside Jarl while lifting his weapon "let's grease them both. What does it matter, she'll just grow up to be one of them anyways, might as well kill her now!"

Something inside Jarl knew immediately that the soldier was dead serious; he was all too familiar with the tone of bloodlust in a man's voice. All sorts of thoughts rushed through his head all at once. Jarl didn't know whether to jump on him, or grab hold of the gun and try to redirect its fire at the ceiling, all he knew was that this innocent child was less than a second away from death and he needed to act! Yet, he stood there, frozen, unable to move. He winced as he watched the machine gun fire rip through the little girl and her captor with such force that pieces of them were literally tacked to the wall behind where they once stood. Rushing over to them and dropping to his knees, he gathered the small child up into his arms, knowing there was nothing he could do for her as the life drained from her body, spilling out with each labored breath. As he rocked back and forth, overcome with grief, she looked up at Jarl, and though she was unable to speak, her eyes seemed to beg the question: "WHY?" So it was that Jarl's brain forced him to relive those terrible moments yet again, and as always, his failure to act left him heart broken and empty.

It was at this point that Jarl became vaguely aware of a voice that sounded like his mother's calling out to him. Opening his eyes, he was somewhat comforted to find her standing there, that same sweet smile that had carried him through many scuffs as a child,
so full of love, and so naïve.

"Come on sweetheart, I made you some supper, it will be good for you to eat."

"I don't really feel like eating right now mom," Jarl said as he propped himself up on his elbows, trying to look and sound normal so that she wouldn't worry.

"Don't be silly Jarlie; you can't hide yourself in here all night, your cousin Sam is here to welcome you home and your father and I would really like to see you. It feels like an eternity since the last time we sat down to a meal together! Besides, I made your favorite: chicken pork chops," she said with a smile that seemed to say 'I won't be taking no for an answer.'

"Alright, mom, for you. I'll be out in a minute."

Watching as his mother left the room; Jarl fell backwards onto the bed. As he stared at the ceiling his vision went blurry and he tried to recall what it was that he had just been dreaming about. All he could remember was a feeling of terror, and he had a fuzzy notion it had something to do with the war. As Jarl stood up from where he lay, and walked towards the door, he couldn't help feeling that he had lost something. His room felt weird, like it belonged to somebody else.

As he walked into the dining room his cousin Samuel jumped up from where he sat, walked over and gave him a hug.

"What's up Jarlie boy? Long time, no see!" offered Sam jovially.

"Hey Sam, yeah it's been awhile hasn't it?"

"Yeah, I was starting to wonder if you were ever coming back, what's it been now, four years?"

"Well, I'd be liar if I told you I hadn't been counting the days."

"You know, Becka has been asking about you quite a bit lately."

"Oh yeah? How is she doing?" asked Jarl, trying to sound as if he cared.

"She's alright, wonders why you stopped writing her though..."

"Couldn't bear to tell her what was happening, the things I'd seen...and done," Jarl stared at the ground as he said this, averting his gaze as if ashamed.

"Well I wish you'd have kept up with it. She's moved on and is dating some big city dude now, met him off to college" Sam replied rolling his eyes.

"That's great Sam, I'm happy for her" Jarl said.

"'Happy for her?' That's your girl, Jarlie, and you let her slip away! Now, she's in the arms of some asshole that you know can't treat her half as well as you did."

"What should I have done differently Sam? Huh? You tell me. I was on the other side of the world, in a war! Besides we were just children."

"Yeah but what you had was real. We all thought sure you two would end up tying the knot. You know, together forever and all that" ventured Sam.

"What do you know about forever? Try living with the notion that everyday is your last, then talk to me about 'forever.' If she's happy, and found real love, then that's all I care. Hopefully we'll all be so lucky."

"If you boys are done with your chit chat, come on over here to the table so we can eat this great lookin' supper your mom threw together for us" said Abe, looking somewhat perturbed. As Jarl and Sam seated themselves at the table, Hazel looked warmly upon all three men and said insistently, "Let's say grace before we eat."

"Our Father, who art in heaven, blessed be thy name. Thank you Lord, for once again bringing us together to share in your bountiful gifts, and thank you for allowing Jarl to come home to us, having served you well. We pray for the young men and women who are still in Iraq, that you might allow them to return safely to their families as you have returned Jarl to us. Please continue to watch over us, and favor us with your love. Bless us this day, in Jesus name we pray - Amen."

Jarl raised his head and smiled at his mother. Even though the last few years had shaken his faith to the point that he found himself wondering how there could be such horrible heartache and sorrow in the world if there really was a God, he found her prayers comforting.

"So Jarlie, what you think about the troop withdrawal everyone keeps talkin' about? You figure we won this war or what?" asked Abe.

"I don't know dad," replied Jarl, somewhat frustrated at the realization that all his father seemed interested in talking about was the war. "I don't know if it's something that can be measured by winning or losing."

"Hah. What's there to even debate about it, we won of course!" piped in Sam with a wink and a mischievous grin. "We wouldn't be leaving if we hadn't. Shit, you ask me we should have just dropped a couple dozen nukes over there and turned that sandbox into a glass bowl know what I mean? Why even bother sending ground troops?"

"That's right Sammy. We showed those sons of bitches a thing or two about what happens when you mess with Lady Liberty!" grunted Abe.

Jarl looked over at his mother, hoping that she would jump in and offer a voice of reason to the conversation, but she just sat there with an expression that reflected her sadness, as she slowly shook her head.

"Come on boy, you got to have some kind of opinion, you just spent the last four years over there" probed Abe in between mouthfuls.

"Yeah what's the big deal Jarlie, cat got your tongue? You can tell us, we're all family here. Shit man, all that laser guided technology and you're sitting here acting like you had to go door to door, wasting little kids and burning down villages..."

On hearing that Jarl threw his fork down on his plate, slid his chair back and abruptly rose up, turning as if to leave. Sam quickly grabbed hold of his arm and looking up at him asked "Where you going?"

"Out. I need some fresh air. Going to get some smokes."

"I'll drive you," Sam offered.
"No thanks, I'd rather walk."

"Man, what is your deal?" Sam inquired, offended.

"Nothing, I just need to be alone right now, OK? I need to think, get my head straight, and that's not happening here."

"What are you doing smoking?" Hazel asked with surprise, "When did you start that?"

"Boy, you better sit down and eat this meal your mother made for you" warned Abe.

Shaking free of his cousin's grasp, and disregarding his father's warning, Jarl grabbed his jacket and with a heavy stride, trudged off. When he reached the door, he flung it wide open and lunged out into the starry night.

Once outside, Jarl labored to put some distance between him and the old house before eventually easing his pace. Gazing up at the night sky, he drew in a long cool breath through his nose, and felt like he could almost smell the stars. There were so many of them up there, and it occurred to him that the sky he was looking at now was the same sky he'd been looking at for the last four years over Iraq. As he walked towards the gas station his thoughts kept wandering back to the stars. He mused that it was entirely possible that each one of those thousands of stars had a solar system of its own, with an Earth-like planet of its own, with intelligent beings; and he wondered if their world was as screwed up as his. If he were somehow able to travel to one of those other worlds, would he find the people there hating and killing each other? Immersed in contemplation, it was not long before he found himself approaching the gas station, and from a distance it looked exactly the way he remembered it. Even the ancient rusted out semi trailer was still parked around back. Entering he expected to be greeted by old Henry, the owner. Instead, to his surprise a dark-complected gentleman stood behind the counter and asked in a low voice accented by a Middle Eastern dialect:

"May I help you?"

"Where is Henry?" Jarl asked confused.

"Henry? Oh, perhaps you would be referring to Mr. Harbinger? I am sorry to tell you that he has passed on from this life. My family and I own this establishment now. Please, is there any way that I might be of help to you?"

Still absorbing the news that Henry Harbinger was dead, Jarl, with his shoulders sunk even lower than usual approached the counter saying "Just give me a couple packs of Camel Lights, please."

As the man turned to grab the cigarettes from the wall behind him, Jarl heard a squealing of tires outside, and turned just in time to see a green Oldsmobile skid to a halt in front of the station. The driver's side door flung open, and a man of athletic build wearing a ski mask jumped out. Jarl's training kicked in and he immediately noticed the man was armed with a hand gun. Before Jarl could say or do anything, the man was shoving his way past the swinging glass door and trained the gun on Jarl, then the attendant.

"Listen up. You two stay calm, and no one gets hurt. You try to call the cops, or do anything I don't like, your both dead. Now, empty the register. NOW!!"

"P-please," stammered the attendant, "I have a family, please, do not hurt them."

"Shut the hell up, and put the cash on the counter. You got ten seconds before I pull this trigger! COME ON, MOVE IT!" shouted the robber. Turning to see Jarl standing within arms reach, hands in the air, he waggled the gun at him indicating that he wanted Jarl to lie down on the ground. Jarl carefully lowered himself down onto the cold floor, as he was overcome with a feeling of deja vu. Everything was happening so fast, he couldn't quite wrap his head around why all this felt so familiar to him. He felt there was something he needed to remember...

Just then a small girl walked into the lobby from behind where Jarl lay, and where the gunman was holding her father within inches of his life. "Daddy, aren't you going to read me a story before bed?" asked the little girl, before realizing that her father had a gun pointed at his head. On recognizing what was happening, she let out a terrified scream, and Jarl immediately connected the dots. It was as if a fog had lifted from his brain. This was his dream, that terrible wicked dream that had been plaguing him for months now, but something was different. Was this Iraq? Was he awake? Was this for real? Time itself seemed to slow to almost a halt as Jarl fumbled for the answers. Straining his neck to peer back towards the girl, he then rolled onto his side to get another look at the gunman. He turned just in time to see the robber take aim at the child. "No-o-o-o-o-o!" came the muffled cry from the father, and something within Jarl snapped. Swallowing hard as every muscle in his body burst with adrenaline, he shoved himself upwards from where he lay prone on the ground, and thrust his body between the child and the gun, shielding her. Reaching out, Jarl clasped both of his hands around the gun and struggled to wrench it free from the assailant. *Ker-r-r-a-ck* thundered the pistol, and Jarl was vaguely aware of the slug as it passed through his stomach, and cracked one of his ribs. Falling to the floor in a heap, he clutched at the gaping hole in his belly with one hand, and the gun with his other. He could feel warm fluids spurting out between his fingers, and it was with great difficulty that he raised the gun, his hand trembling violently, and took aim at the weaponless thug. Realizing his predicament, the would be thief turned on his heels so abruptly that he almost fell face first into the glass door that blocked his retreat. Jarl sat there with the gun aimed at him until he got into his car and had sped some distance away from the station. Certain that they were out of danger he let the gun fall to the floor as he collapsed in a heap. Looking up, he saw the father and daughter embrace, and it suddenly occurred to him that if he were to die then and there, he could die in peace.

As the fluids pooled on the floor beneath him, a strange mixture of blood and bile, Jarl grew light headed. Closing his eyes, he could see his family and friends, and his mind was set adrift in a sea of memory. Suddenly it all became clear to him. It was as if a heavy weight had been lifted from his chest and he could breathe again, and though the air came in gasps and gulps, it was as if he was tasting it for the first time. As he lay there curled up, his thoughts turned to Iraq and the war that had claimed the lives of so many. Some of them close friends, others, total strangers, yet brothers and sisters all, bound for life. Then, just as he was about to slip out of consciousness, he felt two tiny hands reach behind his head, propping it up slightly. With what little strength he had left, he forced his eyes to open, and gazing outward through the tears, beyond the veil of his own mortality, he saw that the child had cradled his head on her lap. He could see that she was crying, and though he was unable to hear her, the words she spoke to him were unmistakable; *"Thank you..."* was the last thing Jarl saw before everything went black.

***

"In other news, in a daring act of heroism, native son Jarl Deaks courageously placed himself between a gunman and a little girl yesterday, during the attempted robbery of an area gas station. Deaks, on leave from his unit in Iraq had just arrived home prior to the shooting. It is unknown what brought Deaks to the gas station last night, but what is certain, is that if not for his intervention, there appears to be a strong possibility that harm would have befallen the child."

Haiku # Seven Hundred and Eight

Do not go my love
Though my actions betray me
My soul longs for you

Charinsa T.

NEGOTIATING COMPROMISES
By April C. Hayes

I.   OMAR ROBERTS

Falling like a torrential downpour, a barrage of thoughts moved through his head like a full-on assault. Images, memories, and questions demanding answers corrupted the morning's meditation. Silent, Omar inhaled deeply, eyes shut, and just listened. To the beating in his heart, he listened. To the song of the Norfolk-Southern screaming wildly in the distance, he listened. Just outside, road workers serenaded the morning with their street opera; a cacophonous racket played annoyingly for those still in bed past 7am. Still, he listened. To the sound of the marble coolness beneath his feet, he listened. He listened to the sounds of his past and the angles of his future.

This moment, *this* was his church, his temple where daily, silent prayer was held, and he nearly reached the place of absolutes when the volatile question pervaded: what do you see? *She had smacked right into the door frame as she exited, elegantly, and he laughed to himself as he rushed to catch up to her. Damn if everything about her wasn't elegant -- her abrupt stance when their interview was over; the way she left the table, evaporating right out of her seat, commanding silk and suede to obey the laws of place. There was the way she turned sharply on tan stilettos, pausing momentarily for her keys, smiling coyly at him over her shoulder, only to cat-walk right out of the restaurant and into a door frame. She played it off beautifully, he thought, taking a soft step back, touching a hand to her chest to laugh at herself obviously. She let it be known she wasn't threatened, nor defeated by a whimsical error, and then she laughed comically upon exiting.*

His morning ritual was poisoned by everything he remembered about her; a soft scar that folded into the corner of her lip, so thin, razor-like, but its presence adorned her with a sincere, childlike quality. Soft, natural curls framed her face like Venetian latticework over laughing eyes. She reminded him of living artwork, a complex canvas in motion; a living sculpture where no wall was good enough.

She took the digital recorder off the table quickly and thanked him. Taken, he leaned toward her, grinned and said, "Ok, my turn. I have a question for you -- just one." Confidently he knew his line would be bitten. Years of cerebral play, in and out of diminutive encounters, had aught him much. After all, she was a reporter, wasn't she? What was it she said? Oh yeah, a humble writer with an in depth in-your-business-complex. Besides, he mused, more than anything, she was a woman. She was a black woman, a bonafide sista, which innately meant a mystical detective. No doubt, she would eagerly want to know what he wanted to know about her.

"I suppose," she replied slowly, to his surprise, carefully smoothing the folds of her skirt as she began to evaporate into the air around him, "I am to be captivated at

the notion that you've got some interest in me." She placed
her hands on the table and leaned into him. *"And, I
suppose,"* she continued, *"this feigned attempt at said
mounting interest is supposed to have me excited with
possibilities."* Omar sat back smoothly, defenseless, to let
her freely cut into him. *"Mr. Roberts, other than doing my
job, this has become...well, in a word...'trite', and I won't
bore you with the details except to say,"* she dropped her
voice to a whisper, *"I'm not interested."* And with that she
smiled coolly, dissolving elegantly into a one-woman play:
up, stop, pause, keys, last look-over-the-shoulder-baby
smile, turn, walk that walk, reigning -- right into the damn
door frame. Though it tickled him, even satisfied him to a
point, he couldn't deny that even out-of-sight, his
atmosphere was consumed with her. Well done, he thought.
She more than heightened his interest, she had clobbered
his sensibilities. She was a killer, he mused, a true,
erotically-witted, dyed-in-the-wool, natural born killer.
Nothing better. He went after her craving a new challenge.
She was formidable, a fortress to be penetrated, but chic
cuisine, not eaten, but savored. A drink never shaken but
gently stirred. She was a new elixir.*

Posing for an invisible audience, Omar praised the
reflection of his looks: espresso-dipped torso blanketed by a
sea of flat, wavy black hair that draped like a silk sheath.
He roughly massaged thick fingers into the short, rib-like
squares in full salute; all six, prized and daily earned;
pulling them in tightly while he stared at himself, picking
apart certain elements. He imagined her all over again.

*He caught up to her waiting at the valet. Moving in
stride, he approached her casually. "In war, Ms. Lambert,"
he said," don't you think it rude not to at least declare
impending doom before firing? I mean, even in the game of
golf they at least yell 'FORE'."*

April C. Hayes

"I suppose you're right, Mr. Roberts," she quipped, smiling nevertheless. "but are we at war?" She asked him this as though she were perched on the precipice of danger ready to leap when necessary. Slyly, the razor-thin scar betrayed that she was feeling him; its softly cragged cut twisted into a cunning smile. She liked him -- he knew it. They bantered about long after her car came, long after his arrived. Two black coffees and dessert -- he insisted -- led to four drinks, jazz and a delectable diatribe at the Carlyle. She was from the Midwest, the Twin Cities, though in her mind there was very little 'twin' about them. He had been to Chicago; had family there. Yeah, she had been to Chicago--often--and regaled him with veritable, impromptu excursions of: cutting out in a stolen Caddy for a weekend with her homegirls 'cause her cousin in Forest Park told her about some party on the Southside, or the time they got caught stealing shit out of Marshall Field's department store and went to jail. Cook County jail! He laughed genuinely when she admitted she "woulda fucked devil cum outta somebody" just to get out, if but one day earlier. They were out one day shy of a week.

Outside of Chicago, he admitted thinking that no other black people existed -- just White Plains, cows and some old-assed Indians. "Native Americans," she corrected him, sweeping his slight ignorance under the rug before telling him she despised pimps. "It's all a game of psychology," he gently argued before leading her to the dance floor. They argued in between sets, her openness jarring, stimulating. Closing time left them hungry, more for the company than food and at 4.a.m. they laughed into their breakfast at Waffle House. She played too tired to argue when he insisted on following her home and they both knew it was game. So ingrained into the fabric of their beings was it, that they couldn't help themselves. She wasn't tired at all. She was electric, imagining herself a killer.

Omar gazed into himself while bending over the sink ever so slightly, pressing his palms into the marbled top, and then, with a hard turn of the knobs, demanded water to splash his face, washing her down his skin. Behind him, the sound of bath water getting away distracted him and he quickly moved to shut it off. Disrobed, naked, open, Omar sought solitude sinking heavily into hot water – *shit, hot!* Yet it felt good, and with the stinging subsiding, his body adjusting to the heat, his thoughts ran amok; and -- *she closed her eyes, smiling softly, smiling coolly, letting the wet from her tongue fall aimlessly onto the head, bowed and kissed the baldness, then drank him in deeply.* Omar, struggling with a losing battle, gave up; *the moment was caramel, hard, soft, sweet and sweat; a beautiful carnival ride; up he went, down she came, then round they went, spinning wildly, spinning out-of-control...*

Steam formed tiny silver glass beads that glittered across his skin, enchanted by recessed lighting. Fully submerged, he traced her smell on him even though it had been two days. Whether she wore oil or perfume he couldn't remember, and really didn't care, but allowed himself enough of her to get carried away in the sweet way the smell of her pussy got mixed up in whatever it was he wore. He surprised himself; this was not at all like him. He had had many women and had, good pussy before, really good pussy so he thought, but DAMN! *She finally answered his one question; what made her want to be a writer? What drove her, moved her, inspired her to put pen-to-paper to create a cocktail of words?* "Hard to answer that," she said. "I guess I'd have to say it's my heart," she surmised; and with the last word, he took her hand, laid it on his chest and said, "Then, you'll understand mine."

This big girl, cool on the retinas, firmly soft up under him, moved into the sound his body was making 'cause fuckin' made good-ass music. He set his eyes wide to watch her while he fucked her, killin' her ass with a kiss; dizzy in her mouth as she sang moans; ached in the way her body bent when he folded her in the palm of his hand: her back, her neck, her head...

Passion getting the better of them, he wanted to fuck her to death right then and there, though with great pains he took his time. Slowly, methodically, he got himself in the creases between leg and the fatness of pussy, opened the fullness of his mouth and placed a watery kiss, tongue extended and moving from one intersection to the next. Her sound, remnant of a muffled giggle, wafted upward over and over again, as he continued to play her music; again, ah, oooo, oh shit! Fingers in her flesh, the battle for supremacy waged. "Ooo baby, yeah there, aaaah, right there, oh, oh—" Getting harder, still, he would wait 'cause right now he was Master -- yeah, of the universe -- and he wouldn't be denied. He would be king.

Looking a good-ass sexy mess, she stretched her arms above her head toward nirvana. Swelling, extending, reaching and multiplying, no void lay between them; only a sliver of light punctuated the darkness. He, imagining it juicy, imagining its fatness, got high. He kissed, sucked, sighed and moved up and down along her rivers edge 'til she conceded death, then moved in for the kill. Mmph, oh shit! Hot water running everywhere; we're fallin' too fast. Yeah, don't stop baby 'cause I'm fuckin' you in this verse, my beautiful, fat-pussied lick. Mmmmm, fuck you nigga, oh just fuck you- good, good, good, baby, baby, baby-- ooooo, oooo, mutha'fucka, ssshhhiiiiiiiiitttt, baby, sshhhhiiiiiitttt! And so the song went.

As their bodies moved together, musical notes inverted for harmony's sake, then she wrapped her legs around him tightly; holding on. Incapable, nor desirous of restraint, he had to look, so he looked - saw himself move above, in and over her; he was a storm, thunder clapping, lighting-cracked sky. He glazed over, a calm, a peaceful riot good inside her. He looked at her again only to be fucked up when she looked back at him, said, "Nigga, this is the best pussy you've ever had", then opened herself more and let his black ass come right in.

Omar didn't shake it. It was a new feeling, one he hadn't experienced before. He confessed himself curious. Question was could he do it? No, never the question of commitment; he was intimate with loyalty, had been baptized a newborn in its waters; understood its demands and perquisites of sacrifice. He had been a street soldier for years, having given over much of his life to its principals and had done many, many things surpassing his emotional content, remembrances that churned and bubbled in disgust -- all in the name of loyalty. Far from anything he knew, from anything he had touched, this was much different. This was untamed abandonment; this was surrender, and therein the puzzle laid an answer and the question.

Now, in this moment, this rigor of solitude, he learned what he saw. Just now, sublimely immersed in the riddle of his life was the answer to the proverb that plagued him. After taking in the sum total of her parts and adding them up, the equation totaled, he confessed, she was the truth. Still, the question begged for its own answer, what was it he saw? There was no denying it, or the first time ever, without mirrors, slight of hand or wizardry, without hiding behind panes of tempered glass; he recognized it in her face, in her movements, in her defense the answer he could no longer deny. For in her, Omar saw himself.

II.   Hearts and Spades

> *A woman easily had*
> *Is a woman easily rid of*
> *A man forgets too soon*
> *What it was that he was after*
> *It all went down so fast*
> *-Unknown*

Just above the dashboard, past the seam where the window's affixed, a scarring of rusted train tracks could easily be seen cutting into Northcrest Road, severing the lower end of the street from its hilly elevation. It was easy to see the tracks, where they ended -- or began, depending on the point of view -- but where they mellowed into the earth was a graveyard of old rail cars left to be forgotten. A city of gray, weather-beaten warehouses filled in the back drop, appearing as cartooned cut-outs against a dimly lit night, making the yard look despondent, lonely...even hurt.

There were four, abandoned rail cars, lined up side by side, mere carnival skeletons of their former years when they muscled cargo from coast-to-coast. Beneath their hulls, stalks of dried mustard weeds and high, yellow grasses sprouted up between them, carpeting their hems like ribbons on little girls' dresses. A sloping, metal fence moped weakly along the yard's access road, which looked more like a pool of water drowning into itself than any offer of protection. And there, behind the iron-railed vista, deep at the base of the access road, marijuana smoke, a thick, grayish waft treaded skyward, completely unnoticed.

Cleverly hidden in a sea of retired grass, deftly secured behind rail, a beautiful, black sedan lay in wait, conspiring in secret. One of the windows was cracked an inch, pouring out smoke from an open wound. Where it was parked, the car had an excellent view of the street where Oakcliff cut across the tracks to become Northcrest, where aging street lamps signaled each other in Morse code. A slim view could be seen of the brick buildings peeking up over the hill, but peripherally to the left, it was easy to see where the trucks rested their tin carcasses at the SINCO station near the mouth of the freeway. But the best view of all was the one right across the street, dead ahead at the Waffle House.

Behind the haze, fingers fumbled nervously, trying to conduct some semblance of restaurant surveillance while trying to wrap up some confidence in a sheath of tobacco. With every pull of the blunt, as the smoke traveled downward, into the lungs, softening the pulse and mellowing the flesh, a wired feeling of confidence grew to an undeniable feeling of supremacy, an unfathomable level of craziness guiding the wheel of an ingenious plot. There would be no apologies for this moment, no reasons for regret, although the fingers constantly drumming nervously did so with contradiction.

This deliciously devious plot was hatched in the smoke-filled belly of the Carlyle. The vile, radical idea took on a life of its own when the shock of a familiar face interrupted what started out as a good time. There was dancing and laughing, laughing and dancing. There were both laughing and dancing together, followed by smiling and dipping. When the temperature reached slow dragging, an invidious plan, one that was particularly yummy, was born. *The sedan tailed them from a safe distance; having waited patiently for them to leave the club's parking deck, making sure to keep far enough away so as not to be noticed by two people falling in love. Behind a shroud of low beams, the car stalked carefully as two, absent of anything else, chased each other in their cars playfully in and out of lanes on Peachtree Road. Flowing in tandem, only observing the speed limit when necessary, they toured new developments and dreamed of posh real estate. By the time they got to Lenox Mall and hailed a left past Phipps, she sent him a 'text' to say that she was hungry. "Me too, baby. Waffle House?" he asked when he called her and they agreed to breakfast. By the time the two reached Northcrest Road, where Oakcliff takes over at I-85, a desperate and determined black sedan made a sharp right turn into a rail storage yard.*

The fingers continued their methodic drumming as the sky began to loosen its grip on the night, freeing itself for the introduction of morning. An unnatural quiet settled into the weighted folds and hand-stitched seams of butter soft leather, followed by an assurance of power that consumed the multi-contour seats, deepened inside the alloy cinder block and fixed itself to the grill's embedded insignia. But all the creature comforts of this beautiful car were woefully oblivious when the waitress across the street served the couple their plates of eggs, bacon and toast. While she refilled glasses of sweet tea, eye wells filled with tears.

She looked for and found the CD she needed and watched as her hand shook while putting the disk into the dashboard stereo. She selected Track 6 as a demand to ease an unforgiving hurt and listened painfully while a trio of women sang heavy woes, their voices sailing high above bass, snare and strings. They sang so hard, of loving hard, that her well of tears overflowed onto a perfectly made up face. They sang of loving men hard; hard men, uncomfortable men to-have-'n'-to-hold and she tried her best to let go of her collapsing heart. And because of their song, she felt understood; felt that someone could get with the immeasurable evil she was ghastly becoming. She figured the women who sang were musical prophets, issuing their warning in a melody. And while she sat there staring at the two having breakfast, three women sang in C at the bottom of their souls, only to lift their tenor to heaven. She put Track 6 on REPEAT and flew once again with the trio of songbirds as they crescendoed over hills and swept low into valleys, singing their rhapsody as theme music to her deadly conclusion.

Inside the Waffle House, a feast of hearts serenaded the perfection of pecan waffles drenched in syrup and mused delectably over the ways to scatter, smother, dice and cover hash browns. At their table, a twenty-something, waitress with way too much gum in her mouth and -- apparently -- way too much time on her hands, stood over her patrons gabbing openly as if they had all gone way, way back. It was not until a throat clearing *"ah hem"* from behind the counter reminding her to move her ass that she cleared the dishes for coffee. When their cups were turned up for decaf (*"really too tired for all that caffeine, though"...and they both grinned, blushed),* and their conversation eased back into a warm neutral, a woman hurt, a woman huddled in the darkness of German craftsmanship stabbed at the CD changer, needing a rap song instead, needing one immediately. So, pain exchanged contrition for conviction and put in 50 Cent.

Music blaring, 50 threatening, revenge watched them as they continued to dance through their food. Two hours she watched through unbelieving eyes and for two hours she waited until she saw them shift toward the door. Good nights were passed around, and, he being "the good guy" he "was 'n all," picked up everyone's tab even though three other people actually ate. The gentleman at the counter, bowing under the weight of his years only had coffee. Still, everyone thanked him sincerely, and he, being sincere himself, convinced the writer to let him get close, despite their earlier slow drag to a jazz-funk rendition of *"Teach Me Tonight,"* both silently agreeing to be Master and apprentice.

He placed his hand at her back and gingerly escorted her to her car. And when he bent her head toward him with both hands and laced her with a forehead kiss, time fell into a warp between their two cars and anyone within a mile of the two, anyone incognito behind an abandoned train, could see they wouldn't end *there* in *that* parking lot. They were seriously caught in deep waves of electricity -- bright, bright lights -- and unbeknownst to them, their fire ignited a jealousy that hath no scorn.

Unbeknownst to them, an avalanche of tears came, rolling down the face of a defeated soldier. They rained as penance and flowed as rage, poured out as an offering up to God. Only, did he have to put his hands on both sides of her face; hold her lovingly, as if she were ancient china? Holding her there as if she would break, as if in that moment, he could lose her?

She barely understood jealousy, having never felt it herself. She was accustomed to being the purveyor of envy, the supplier of hate, had always enjoyed a loftier view of first place admiration, until now. Had she known, or if anyone had ever spoken to her about it, she never listened, for had she, she would've know what most mothers tell their daughters' at the spring of new breasts. She would've known barmaid tales and tavern prose of men whose feet never touched the face of the earth again because the hand of a jealous woman trembled in pain. Then, she would've understood that the song she coveted, the song she believed was prophecy wasn't prophecy at all. Then she would've intimately understood that the song she listened to in that car, the one with the ménage `a trois of voices crushed from the same jealousy, was an all too familiar song.

And when the longest kiss-goodnight lingered, a torpedo of molten lava superseded any common sense within the sedan's dark doors and a vibrant pain flashing bright crimson exploded beneath a hand of woven cotton, hidden in the shadows, behind a vacant, sleeping train.

III.   Cecile Lambert

6:38 a.m.

"Nightcap?" Cecile asked, gliding, keys out for the door. A light breeze dipped into their conversation knitting them closer together and they hardly marveled that it had taken less than 20 minutes to get to her place.

"Don't need it," he kidded, nudging her gently inside. There they made soft noises, mashing each other into walls as to become human graffiti; forever plastered into a comic strip along her narrow corridor.

"So, no nightcap?" She dusted his ear lightly.

"No," he kissed her, "no nightcap."

6:54 a.m.

Lost in infinite, finite space; where was she, the bed, the floor? She didn't know. Time? She didn't care 'cause he was thinning out her thick places, having already smoothed her rough edges.

8:41 a.m.

Peonies, she imagined an endless, brilliant field of peonies: Sorbets, Raspberry Sundaes, Purple and Pink trees; Bowls of Beauty floating on puffs of air, High Noons bathing in petulant rays, while Shirley Temples fragrantly bobbed their heads. In bed, she lay floating to her body's music, drifting in the symphonic breathing of the man next to her, daydreaming of peonies. With her fingers, she retraced him, touching the places he had touched, imagining the same creases, tors and tufts of flesh, gelatin at his request. On a gale, her heart danced calypso when he pulled her into him without waking.

11:03 a.m.

A stream of sunlight broke across the bay of windows, peering in on wrangled bodies, twisted and tormented in bliss.

1:11 p.m.

By the time the sun reached its apex to spit on the equator, cyclists, joggers, walkers and strollers paraded doggedly through Grant Park, narrowly dodging kicked balls, runaway toddlers and spontaneous canines. Saturdays at the park were typically full of suburban exiles: mothers retreating mundane expectations, fathers escaping adolescent tactics, both hoping to preserve any civility of sanity. This was their oasis, a mini-paradise where, if, but for a few minutes, they could relinquish themselves to a municipality of nature, or at least enjoy a bit of devilment by dumping little ones on a sullen teenager. Barbeque grills sending up smoke flares dotted the park and a hop, skip and jump away was Zoo Atlanta. And, Cecile's balcony opened up to all of it.

For her, mornings on the deck accompanied by a cup of coffee was an immeasurable pleasure, communing with the story-telling trees that canopied the outskirts of the park, especially since her stretch of Cherokee was absolutely breathtaking. Cecile yawned into Omar's ear and slowly whispered, "I got coffee, baby. I got...Blue Hawaiian -- which is my favorite, some Kenyan, Columbian – oh, and there might be a "skoche" of Starbuck's Bold."

"A skoche?"

"Yeah, nigga, a skoche," she giggled holding a forefinger and thumb slightly apart to show she meant 'a bit'.

"Ok, whatever," he smirked. "C'mere, skoche," and he wrapped himself up in her, vibing to the marching staccato under her tits resounding in the fullness of her belly Her arms circled him naturally.

"So, now that we're awake," he propped and molded pillows for more support, "let me tell you about *the Maunder Minimum*--"

"What? The what?"

"*The Maunder Minimum*," he repeated. "It's a little known fact about the sun, otherwise known as the 'Little Ice Age'," he said proudly, gently repositioning the arm that fell asleep cradling her head. Launching into a fully awakened conversation, he told her about the sun's output not being entirely constant, that sometime during a millennium, the sun atypically ceased to produce sunspots; and wasn't it amazing that something so bright, so powerful, so necessary for the existence of man could actually run cold -- he saw it on the Discovery Channel. Cecile could tell his cerebral engine was revving now, and, in a minute she would have to get completely up.

"This scientist, this guy named Edward Maunder discovered it when studying..."

"Omar," she interrupted.

"Baby?"

"Does this mean you want coffee or no?" Emitting a slight, throaty giggle, she was irritatingly tickled by his sudden spurt of alertness and nonstop, excitable drone of scientific data. Incessantly, he preached about how the sun emitted these solar winds, which was really a low density stream of charged particles (mostly electrons and protons) that, when impacting the earth in certain seasons created the mesmerizing *aurora borealis*, otherwise known as the Northern Lights. Was he serious? Not that she was uninterested in him, what he was saying or even the fact that he was saying it -- she was interested in all of him. Hell, she was even interested in the 'Northern Lights', but, when it came to sleep, rest, me time/we time in her bed –

well -- some things just took precedence. So she figured, before he said or did anything else to keep her awake in their solar system, especially since caffeine wasn't involved, that he had to shut up or she was gonna end up punching him in his Southern Hemisphere.

"You must really love coffee," he muffled. "What're you, Starbucks?" His grin stretched a mile across his face as he slid down onto her and further into the covers.

"Well, I know *that* ain't Starbucks," she sent an elbow to his ribs, and the offer of robust Columbian waned as she felt his hand slip between her legs.

4:08 p.m.

A showering of paling leaves wept over Castleberry Hill when Omar left Cecile re-fastening a disheveled robe. The backdrop was floral, fauna when they lingered with their goodbyes at the door. It seemed an eternity between her and the chance to relive the amazement of yesterday -- meeting him at Vinali's in Buckhead, ending up at club Carlyle -- and up until a few minutes ago, her return from this morning's Utopian universe.

Grinning to shame a jack-o-lantern, she pulled the robe tighter around hips that sang; only her ears heard the music and her lips played it. She laughed at herself, at the zephyr wind she rode uncaringly, safely and surprisingly, considering they just met. She felt at ease with him, moved with him. Like water in a faucet, he poured her out into ravines, spilling her soul into lakes and streams. He made her the Mississippi and her life opened to him wide as the Caspian Sea. Soaring on clandestine wings like the winds across the Sahara, she breezed on tiptoes lightly through her corridor, her heart gushing forth like Lake Victoria, and she laughed when she saw that they had knocked shit everywhere. Two Kissee stoned eggs rested against the base board under the teak settee after saving themselves from being flung against the wall. Her miniature Atlanta Jazz Festival print, the first picture she ever framed, peeked from behind an Ebony wood pedestal and *damn, damn, damn,* the three priceless Varner Betts stick figures, the result of a three year sibling moratorium, 'cause she inherited them from Lola Renee, went toppling onto the floor.

Carefully she lifted each figure, tender as children she examined, tested their parts: Blue Man's thread still wove through his metal bones. His blue, twig hat still cut across his head. Harlem and Bucky Twine's brown and red strings still attached to their copper wiring. She put each one back in their original place, back in order to tame Lola Renee and the massive guilt she carried like a sentence. Besides, she wasn't ready to confront the haunting mother who preached privileges for the pedigreed and waste for sinners. No, Ms. Lola Renee Lambert would wait with her sentence of guilt. Instead, she padded through to the kitchen, pulled a grinder from the pantry, got the skoche of Bold out the freezer, measured 2 ½ cups of water and made herself a strong pot. Coffee brewing, she opened the refrigerator for something to take the edge off when she remembered her leftover, partially-eaten waffle from earlier, which she stuck in the microwave then picked up the phone and dialed Mozelle.

"Oh Ceese, baby, I'm so glad you called. I got a situation...I...this just can't be happening!" cried Mozelle at the other end of the phone. Quietly, Cecile wrestled the phone beneath her chin, pulled out a chair and took a seat. Her brightly colored kitchen suddenly became mute, flavorless, as if the colors turned down their halo in sadness. A sadness that Cecile felt had no business there considering.

"Honey, if this is all about Memphis -- maybe it's not an ending, but, but a beginning." She adjusted the phone in order to eat her bits of waffle. It was a hopeful gesture full of hopeful words. Hopeful in the sense that since, Cecile could remember, since the minute she met the funny, midnight-black girl with a designer chip on her shoulder, since Freshman Orientation, Mo had a critical addiction for all the wrong men and Memphis Smalls, to Cecile, was the worst of them.

Memphis Smalls was a man of simple complexities, a mixed breed. He was strikingly handsome and wretchedly unattractive, charmingly conversational though horribly ignorant and easy to get along with, yet hard to please. Whether coming or going, for Mozelle he was an insatiable pleasure inextricably bound to insane pain. She loved him past his faults, despite his sins and regardless of his intentions. She loved him despite the fact that he made her miserable and instead of loosing him like a bad spirit, like many women, she held herself together tightly for a man she hoped would eventually see her, which ultimately meant he would come to love her. And he did love her, but for the things she did, making sure she appreciated it. For the boulangerie of intricate dinners, he was thankful. For the subtle gifts guised in books, CDs and the occasional concert, he said, *"Preciate you, baby."* For the transitional month he crashed at her crib, no questions asked, he was grateful and, of course, for the three plus years of willing pussy, on her knees, on her back, on the couch, the bed, he came gratefully.

"We're sitting in my car and he just starts talkin' about this woman, some 'friend' of his." Mozelle whined, making Cecile wish she had confronted Lola's demons, or at least gone and got back in the bed with last night's phantoms. "He just sat there talkin' to me as if the last coupla years never happened. I...I can't....begin to tell you....how much it hurts," Mozelle's voiced cracked the walls and splintered the air between them. Cecile's heart went out to her friend, though she had difficulty finding her voice seeing that after three years of this, there wasn't much else to say. So, she said *'yes'* and *'I know'* or *'I understand'* between heavy sniffs and silent pauses.

"Man, Cece, you never see it from the beginning," she blurted. "The end. You never see the end from the beginning."

"The end to exactly what, baby?"

"TO EVERYTHING!" she yelled, assuming Cecile wasn't listening. "Like you don't know how it is," she stammered. "To everything; the end to his anxious smile, you know, the one you got back 'n the day when he was happy to see you, talk to you, fuck you. Shit, you don't even begin to think about the river of love you're gonna pour out for that mutha'fucka just 'cause he said you were his kind of ride-or-die chick. And instead of him lovin' you back the way you're lovin' him -- no, no you get an avalanche of hurt in return."

Mozelle was a sista who sought mortal comfort in the solitude of right angles, exact measurement, placement and distance. None of this spiritual crap, none of that popularized Feng Shui bull, she craved numerical balance, and if all things being equal needed everything to be even. So to be this torn up behind a man who entered and exited at the same time, a man who walked up when others went down, the devil's favorite advocate, to Cecile defied simple understanding. And the truth was she didn't want to understand, not today anyway, not after sailing on a sea of hair like silk with a man that made her dream wildly of sweet peonies.

"I could sure use your company today, Ceese."

"Mo, I dunno, honey. I gotta get Lyle my draft first thing Monday, and to be honest, I'm really just gettin' up..."

Mozelle heard none of that. "Please, I'll cook. I'd do it for you"

Cecile sighed. It was going to be a long day. And while the thought of listening to Mozelle pour on about Memphis instead of Omar coloring the conversation -- well, not having to cook was working in the plus column.

"I know, honey, I know. Gimme a minute to pull it together and I'm out the door." She put the phone down and stuck a finger in cold coffee, mindlessly swirling the liquid around in the cup 'til it made a tiny whirlpool in the center and sighed. This was definitely going to be a long day.

5:36 p.m.

Stepping out into the day, Cecile drew in a snatch of fresh air and marveled at how beautiful the downtown skyline looked. Tops of skyscrapers prayed under a banner of lazy gauze; thinning clouds playing merry-go-round the sun and she smiled for the Northern Lights.

Leaving Castleberry Hill, Cecile drove to the end of her driveway and waited for her turn to get onto Cherokee, when a beautiful, black Mercedes passing slowly, stopped and parked. Cecile admired the slickness of the car, its clean, streamlined design. It amazed her how it appeared to be floating in place though it wasn't moving and she wondered about the driver, about the person who could command such a powerful machine, one she dreamed of one day owning. Believing him to be some CEO, high-paying VP or politician, she was happily surprised when a well dressed, extremely attractive black woman got out and planted two expensively-heeled feet right onto Cherokee.

Soon

soon, I say
soon, he sighed
soon we'll play
soon, I lied
soon, he implored
soon, said I
soon? he asked
soon. I replied
soon, he smiled
yes, said I

Saadia Ali Aschemann

Note to Reader: This poem is an example of **_anaphora_** which is
a poetic term for when the beginning of each line in a poem
repeats the same word or phrase. In the above poem, the
repetition of the words 'soon' at the beginning of each line but the
last suggests obsession. In many anaphoras, the last line or two
of the poem begins with a different word--leading the reader to
believe that the poet's fixation has been remedied.

Prom Queen's Lament

When he's away
he tells me that he
misses

the hollow of my neck
and the length of my legs
the dark of my hair
and the white of my teeth
I love the way you look
                (he tells me)
I wish
that he missed
the strength of my thoughts
and my keen wit
the push of my belief
and the pull of my words

I want him
to tell me
that he misses
        (that he loves)
my mind

Saadia Ali Aschemann

REDEMPTION

payback not purchase
vengeance, vindication
bad times can't erase
sweet salvation

love me then
hate me now
where and when
what and how

deliverance not doubt
redeem, rescue
forceful, a shout
triumph is true

my word: not maybe
victory is sweet
swagger back baby
haters retreat

Saadia Ali Aschemann

About the Contributors

Saadia Ali Aschemann aka Girly-Girl - Saadia Ali Aschemann is a poet and the author of _lavish lines/luscious lies_. She has a Bachelor's Degree from George Mason University and a Master's in Education from the University of Illinois at Springfield. Aschemann lives with her husband and two sons in West-Central Illinois.

www.saadiaonline.com

Diane Dorce' aka Mizrepresent- Diane Dorcé was born and raised in Gary, Indiana. The author of three acclaimed books, _Loving Penny- 2001, Devil In the Mist – 2005,_ and her latest release _52 Broad Street._ She currently lives in Atlanta where she is working on her next novel. Ms. Dorce' is an up and coming writing sensation, and has appeared at various conferences, most recently the 2007 BEA. She has been selected as one of the featured authors at the 2008 Book Club National Convention to be held in Atlanta, GA where she resides as a native.

www.readingwritingblogging.blogspot.com
www.dianedorce.com

R. Fitzgerald aka Mega Rich - is a native Floridian and current resident of St. Louis, MO. He is happily married to his wife of 12 years and has 5 beautiful children. Having spent most of his professional career as a Programmer/Analyst, the University of Florida graduate has found a renewed sense of purpose as he embraces his love for writing. The burgeoning author is currently working on multiple writing projects that represent a diverse set of genres. He anticipates releasing an anthology of Christian fiction short stories and his first novel in 2008.

www.the-rich-house.blogspot.com

Cedric Harris aka The Master (De) bater - is owner of Words Apart Editing "Where Your Words Become Classic Literature and Legendary Speech". Cedric currently resides in San Diego, CA.

www.wordsapart.com
www.worldofwonderworkingpower.blogspot.com

April C. Hayes aka Literary Felonies -April C. Hayes, better known as *"April C"*, is a freelance writer currently residing in Atlanta and much to parental chagrin refuses to leave. April has published a number of articles for magazines and newspapers and has collaborated on two plays. She is currently at work on two novels, *Negotiating Compromises and There Comes A Day.*

www.literaryfelonies.blogspot.com

D.R. Johnson aka Dave J – D.R. Johnson is an aspiring writer currently pursuing his BA in Professional Writing through the Department of Writing, Rhetoric and American Cultures at Michigan State University. Having spent more than a decade in the workforce, David decided it was time for a change, and returning to college, has set about reinventing himself. "The Mending" is his first national writing release. An avid blogger, Mr. Johnson has turned what started as just another way to practice his writing, into a dedicated passion.

www.thewanderingether.blogspot.com

Denea Marcel – is an expressionist artist and writer. She earned her Bachelor's Degree in Comprehensive Studio Art from Hampton University. An advocate of art education for children, Denea has participated in a number of non-profit children's art programs and visited classrooms in Los Angeles to provide art classes for students who would not have otherwise had the opportunity to engage in the arts. She is a lover of life and a constant student. Denea Marcel currently resides in Miami, Florida.

www.thegallerymarcel.blogspot.com

Cordenia Paige aka Capcity – A proud native of our Nation's Capital City, Cordenia Paige moved to New York City in August of 2001. She taught in prestigious private schools in Washington, DC and New York City for sixteen years. Cordenia's experience teaching grade levels PK to 12th grade focused on Humanities, Social Studies and Computer skills. She encouraged her students to take the risks to pursue their dreams and to live passionately. Cordenia is now taking her own advice and loving every demanding step. Cordenia lives in The Bronx where she is at work on a novel, several short stories and educational material. With the help of The Creator her next labor of love will be published in 2008. You can view samples of her writings and musings at:

www.capcity4privateyes.blogspot.com

Torrance Stephens PhD aka All-Mi-T - Mr. Stephens is a writer, poet, essayist, columnist, educator and doctor by trade. His insightful and sometimes hilarious, but always real articles has attributed to his non-traditional fame, attracting readers and fans from all walks of life, across the country. His work has appeared in print and publications such as NOMMO, Creative Loafing, Rolling Out (circulation approx. 1.5 million), Talking Drum, the North Avenue Review and other periodicals. Dr. Stephens has successfully published over 2 dozen articles in Medical Journals and reviews covering such range of topics as HIV risks, AIDs, Homelessness, and Sexual behavior amongst AA college students. He has a huge following both within the academic community and outside. His travels outside of the US have garnered an international following as he continues to dedicate his life to improving the life of others. Stephens, a graduate of Hamilton High School (Memphis, TN), later attended Morehouse College where he studied, Psychology, Biology and Chemistry. He received a Master's degree in Educational Psychology and Measurement from Atlanta University and a PhD. in Counseling from Clark Atlanta University.

On The B-Side...

The writers in this section are talents that we found along the road to publication. Rather than waiting to debut their talent in a future volume, we asked them to make a small contribution to the theme, Love and Redemption.

Orande Ash

Blogger ID:	BYGPOWIS
Location:	Raleigh, NC
Blog Title:	James, Mos Def, My brotha, and me

Blog Profile: I was consumed by "the fire next time," James Baldwin inspired me to write about the burning this time and alight my future.

Blog URL   www.bygpowis.blogspot.com

Donald Smith

Blogger ID:	Don
Location:	Jackson, MS
Blog Title:	Minus the Bars

Blog Profile: The labeling of a snitch is a lifetime scar you will always be in   jail...just minus the bars

Blog URL   http://minusthebars.blogspot.com

Charinsa T.
Blogger ID: MysTery
Location: Houston, TX
Blog Title: Journey to Reinvention

Blog Profile: ~ I am so many things, I can't even
                      begin to explain. Perhaps this may
                      provide a little insight... This is my
                      journey. ~

Blog URL   http://mystery2you.blogspot.com/

Brandy L. McCrary
Blogger ID: Xcentric Pryncess
Location: Lithia Springs, GA
Blog Title: Xcentric Pryncess

Blog Profile:

                      Me with hips and nice sized
                      lips, different from what you say
                      is beauty. Me...you can sit two drinks
                      on what is behind me...You are drunk
                      on this beauty. Unable to focus...
                      Inebriated with me. You say...
                      Straight hair, white skin, thin.
                      I say, whatever. He made you to be.
                      Then be... Just be. Be.
Blog URL   http://xcentricpryncess.blogspot.com